Aberdeenshire

COUNCIL

Aberdeenshire Library and Information Service
www.aberdeenshire.gov.uk/libraries
Renewals Hotline 01224 661511

JUSTIN RICHARDS

THE
SCHOOL OF
NIGHT
CREEPING TERROR

faber and faber

First published in 2011
by Faber and Faber Limited
Bloomsbury House
74–7 Great Russell Street
London WC1B 3DA

Typeset by Faber and Faber Limited
Printed in England by Bookmarque, Croydon, UK

The right of Justin Richards to be identified as author of this work has
been asserted in accordance with Section 77 of the Copyright, Designs
and Patents Act 1988

A CIP record for this book
is available from the British Library

ISBN 978-0-571-24509-3

In the fifteenth century, an alchemist called Gabriel Diablo sought to summon a mighty demon: Mortagula. He thought that if he could control the demon he would be the most powerful man on earth.

But the agents of the Memento Mori stopped him and took away the five Artefacts that he needed to summon the demon:

- 🦂 a Dagger to control Mortagula.

- 🦂 an Amulet which could open a Gateway to Hell and allow the demons to enter our world.

- 🦂 a Crystal that focuses energy to control or harness the forces of darkness.

- 🦂 The Book of Darkness Rising – Diablo's own notes on how he planned to summon the demon.

- 🦂 The Book of Lost Souls – an ancient book of instructions for controlling demons and the dead.

In 1729, the Pope dissolved the Memento Mori and its surviving members went into hiding. What happened to the Artefacts remains a mystery.

If anyone gathered together the five Artefacts, they would have the power to summon forth the demon Mortagula – to control or to destroy the world.

Luckily, the Artefacts have remained lost and hidden . . . until now.

CREEPING TERROR

1

THEY WERE LOST, IT WAS GETTING DARK AND the ghosts were leaving town.

A long line of them, pale in the dying light of the sun, walked towards the car. One man pushed a wheelbarrow laden with boxes. Another was carrying his small daughter. A woman held the hands of two toddlers, their faces smudged and indistinct. All of them looked grim and resigned.

'Who are they all?' Tommy wondered out loud.

'What's that?' his dad said, oblivious to the figures. 'Did you see someone?'

Usually the ghosts were not as distinct. Usually they were just vague shapes and Tommy had to use his mobile phone to see them properly – the special phone he'd been given when he joined the 'extra maths' group. They did some maths, just to keep up the pretence. But the three gifted students were actually learning all about the ghosts and demons, the Grotesques and the spirits . . . Their tutor,

Mr Fothergill, worked for the School of Night.

'It's nothing,' Tommy said. 'Nobody. Have you worked out where we are yet?'

His dad sighed. 'Well, somewhere between Bournemouth and Wareham, I think. We must reach a main road, or at least a signpost, soon.'

Tommy nodded. Dad had been saying that for nearly half an hour.

Making sure it was angled so Dad couldn't see the screen, Tommy flipped open his phone. The last few figures walking along the side of the road shimmered and glowed on the screen, their features sharper and more focused, their auras clearly visible like white haloes. Then the road was empty again. In the distance there was something else – another faint glow. A tall building, like a castle or . . .

'There's a church,' Tommy said. He snapped the phone shut and slipped it back into his pocket. 'Look – over to the left.'

'At last. Civilisation. There'll be signs there. Or if not we can ask.'

The road swung round in a wide bend towards the distant church tower. Silhouetted against the red glow of the sunset, the tower looked ragged and lopsided. Tommy squinted, trying to see it properly, to make out the details.

'I think it's just a ruin,' he said. 'We're in the middle of nowhere.'

'Don't say that. There must be something.'

The church tower disappeared behind trees. Dad turned on the car headlights and at once they shone across something white beside the road up ahead.

'There's a sign.'

Dad slowed right down so they could read it. The sign was pitted and discoloured with age. The paint had faded and one side was broken.

'"Welcome to . . ."' Tommy began to read.

Under those words was the name of the village they were entering. But the letters had been painted out with thick, careless black strokes.

'Vandals,' Dad muttered. 'Nothing's safe these days. Kids probably.'

'I blame the parents,' Tommy joked.

Dad grinned. 'You're probably right at that.'

He was happier now they'd found somewhere. From the moment he realised they were lost, he'd been snapping at Tommy as if it was his fault.

Ahead of them Tommy could see a row of houses. They passed a street lamp – old-fashioned, with a lantern rather than a modern bulb at the top. Like they were driving into Narnia. There was a phone box too. At least, Tommy thought it was a phone box – a small hut with large glass windows. But he thought old phone boxes were red, and this one was dark brown.

The church was visible again, at the far end of the village. Tommy could see now that it didn't look ruined at all. He must have imagined that.

'Pub,' Dad announced. 'Just the place. Funny . . .' he added as he slowed down. 'No other cars about.'

'Maybe everyone's in the pub,' Tommy said.

'There must be a car park somewhere. Not to worry. We're not staying.' He pulled up at the kerb.

They got out of the car and Dad locked it. The pub was on the other side of the road. A sign outside read 'The Green Man'. It showed a picture of Robin Hood, dressed in Lincoln green and holding his longbow.

'Rude just to go in and ask where we are. Might as well have a swift half while we're here,' Dad decided. 'And a Coke,' he added quickly.

'We might not have to,' Tommy told him. 'Someone's coming.'

At first he thought she was another ghost, but Dad obviously saw her too. The elderly lady was leaning heavily on a wooden stick and her white hair was tied back with a black ribbon. The last rays of the sun picked out all the lines in her tired-looking face and made her pale eyes glitter as she peered up at them.

'The green,' she said. Her voice was as old and cracked as her face.

'Yes,' Dad agreed. 'We were just going in. But maybe you can help? We're a bit lost. Need to get back to the A350. I think we missed a turn somewhere.'

The woman nodded thoughtfully. 'We'll all be lost soon.'

'If you could just point us towards the main road,' Dad tried.

The woman turned away, her face falling into shadow. 'Beware the green,' she said as she made her way slowly down the road, fading into the gathering darkness.

'Well, that was helpful,' Tommy said.

'We don't like strangers here,' Dad told him, in a mock West Country accent. 'Let's hope they make more sense in the pub. It'll be dark in a few minutes.'

The street lamps weren't on and nor were the lights in any of the houses so far as Tommy could see. No lights anywhere. Just the faint sound of organ music coming, he guessed, from the church.

'You'd think they'd turn the street lamps on,' Dad said, echoing Tommy's thoughts.

The pub too was in darkness. But there was noise coming from inside. Muffled voices, the chink of glasses, someone singing out of tune.

The noise died away when Dad opened the door. The lights were on inside, but thick, dark blinds were pulled down over the windows. There were bare, round wooden tables on a stone floor and a large middle-aged woman stood behind the bar. Half a dozen men were seated at different tables. Two of them played dominoes. Another two men stood at the long wooden bar. They were all middle-aged or older.

'Don't stand there with the door open,' one of the men at the bar said loudly. 'You'll have old Pearson down on us like a ton of bricks if he sees a light.'

Tommy closed the door and followed his dad to the bar. There were several old-fashioned beer pump handles, and behind the bar he could see a row of bottles and a couple of wooden barrels with taps attached. *Olde Worlde*, Dad would call it.

'You on leave?' the other man at the bar asked.

'Weekend break,' Dad said. 'Just passing through. Er, hoping for directions actually. Oh, and a drink of course,' he added quickly as the woman behind the bar glared at him.

'More trouble than it's worth, getting rid of all the signposts,' the woman said. 'What'll you have?'

'Half of bitter, please.'

'Same for the lad?'

'Oh, God, no. His mum would kill me.'

'Coke?' Tommy asked.

The woman stared at him blankly. Then her face cleared. 'Oh, sorry, love. Don't do hot drinks. No cocoa just now. I'll get you a lemonade if you want.'

Tommy had never heard of a pub that didn't do Coke or Pepsi. But there was something strange about this place, he could feel it, so he just said, 'Fine, yes. Thanks.'

'Which way do I go to get back to the A350?' Dad asked as the woman pulled his half-pint.

'You what?' the first man who'd spoken to them said.

'Main road? Dorchester?'

'Oh, right. You did get lost, didn't you?'

'Out past the church,' the other man told them. 'Turn left at the crossroads, then on over Hooper's Hill and past Home Farm. You'll hit the main road after a couple of miles. Turn right for Dorchester.'

'Unless you're spies, of course,' the first man said, laughing. 'In that case turn right and drive on till you end up in the sea.'

'Lucky you didn't get lost next week,' the woman said when she'd finished laughing with the men. She put a glass of cloudy lemonade in front of Tommy. 'Be no one here to help you then.'

'Just the soldier boys,' the first man agreed. 'Moving us out, they are.'

'I'm sorry?' Dad said, sipping his beer.

'We've been *commandeered*. The whole village has. For the duration,' the second man told them. 'Manoeuvres. Training. Who knows? But they're moving us all out to Clifferton come Tuesday. God alone knows what'll happen to this place.'

'Can they do that?' Tommy asked. 'I mean, just shift people on?' It sounded rather extreme and unfair.

The woman laughed. 'There's a war on, you know. They can do anything they want.'

Dad and Tommy stared at each other. Dad forced a smile.

'What do I owe you for the drinks?' He pulled out his wallet.

'Half of best and a lemonade,' the woman said. 'That'll be fivepence ha'penny.'

Dad was concentrating on the road ahead, his hands tight on the steering wheel.

'Bonkers, the lot of them,' he announced after a while. 'Completely, utterly crazy. "Don't you know there's a war on?" I mean, what's her problem?'

Tommy didn't reply. He didn't think they were crazy.

Dad went on, 'I thought that big guy was going to thump me when I offered the woman a twenty-pound note. Come on! Twenty quid for a couple of drinks?'

'She only wanted five and a half pence.'

Dad shook his head. 'Fivepence ha'penny. That's old pence. You know, as in shillings-and-pence pence. Crazy people. Must be some village pageant or something. He said left at the crossroads, didn't he?'

'Yes,' Tommy agreed.

The road narrowed after the turning. High hedges rose on either side. They were so close together that the car lights shone down both sides at once, illuminating twin walls of green.

'You sure it was left? This doesn't look like the main road.'

Tommy had his phone out. He didn't like what he was seeing on the screen. The hedges themselves seemed to glow on the display panel. He could feel the tightness in his stomach that he always got when there was something strange happening. Something spooky . . .

At the bottom of the phone, slightly recessed so you wouldn't press it by accident, was a red button. Tommy's thumb explored the indentation, then pressed. He held the phone up, knowing that the images it captured were being sent directly to the main computers at the School of Night. They would also be able to retrieve the images that he'd seen earlier. Everything was recorded and stored.

There was something else odd about the hedges on the display panel. It took Tommy a few moments to work out what it was. They didn't seem solid. At least, not where they closed in on the car. Through the translucent vegetation, the road was wider. Yet, looking up and through the windscreen, the road seemed to be narrowing still further. The parts of the hedge that were only vague shapes on the screen looked all too real through the windscreen.

Dad was braking. 'This can't be right. But it's too narrow to turn round and I'm not reversing a mile or more.'

'Just keep going, Dad.'

The road was narrowing more quickly now. The hedges pressed in. Even though the car was travelling at the same speed, the gap was disappearing fast. It was as if the hedges were actually moving.

Actually *moving*?

Tommy double-checked his phone. If he ignored the hazy, ethereal hedges, then the road was still as wide as it should be. Plenty of room. Yet very real leaves were slashing against the window beside him. A branch smacked into the windscreen, leaving a star-shaped crack.

'Faster!' Tommy yelled. He had to shout above the sound of the hedges scraping down the side of the car. 'Keep going!'

Out of instinct rather than logic, Dad accelerated. The sensible thing to do was to stop the car. But somehow they both knew that if they did that the vegetation would close in and smother them.

The dark leaves pressed against the windows. The headlights were dimming, struggling to shine through the mass of branches.

'Left!' Tommy shouted. 'Turn left now!'

'There's a hedge,' Dad yelled back.

There wasn't on Tommy's phone. At least, there was only a suggestion of a hedge, and through it he could see a side turning, a narrow lane leading off the wider road.

'We can get through. Just turn!'

The windscreen went black. There was a loud crack as a branch connected. Scraping and scratching down the side of the car. The roar of the straining engine.

Then sudden moonlight. A country lane ahead of them – white line clear and Cat's-eyes shining in the middle of the tarmac. The car was hurtling towards a sharp bend. Dad wrenched the wheel again and the car skidded into a slide before fishtailing. It righted itself, the wheels caught on the road surface and they were speeding down the lane.

The fields on either side were empty and dark behind the low hedgerows.

Dad laughed. Soon Tommy was laughing too.

'Must have been a farm track. Disused probably. I bet they sent us that way on purpose. Don't you think, Tommy?'

He didn't. 'Yes, Dad.'

There was a figure in the road ahead. A man in uniform with his hand up, waving to them to stop. Tommy checked on his phone. There was no glow, no sign of anything unusual. Just a soldier caught in the main beam of the headlights.

Dad slowed, opening the driver's window. 'There a problem?'

'This road is off limits to civilians, I'm afraid. You're just coming up to an official military checkpoint, sir.'

Tommy could make out a small hut and a barrier further along the road. There were several more soldiers too, and a Land Rover.

'I'm not sure we can get back that way. It's a bit . . . overgrown,' Dad told the soldier.

He glanced down the road, looking puzzled. 'I don't think you understand me, sir. The road you are *on* is off limits. You're approaching our checkpoint from the restricted side. You shouldn't be here at all.'

'Sorry. We got lost.'

The soldier looked across at Tommy. 'Just the two of you, is it?'

'We want the road to Dorchester,' Tommy said. 'We didn't mean to trespass or anything.'

The soldier nodded. 'I'll tell them to let you through. Don't know how you got inside the cordon, there's all sorts of exercises going on out there. Lucky you didn't get caught up in them. You must have been driving for a while . . .'

'It seemed like forever,' Tommy said.

The soldier jogged along, keeping pace with the car as Dad drove it slowly up to the barrier.

'This will take you back to the main road. Turn right for Dorchester, OK?' He looked back the way they had come. 'Lucky you found the road out. You could have been lost in there for ages. There's nothing back that way except Templeton.'

'We drove through it,' Dad said.

The soldier was talking again before he could say anything more. 'Sad place, isn't it? Run down and abandoned. They evacuated it you know, back in the war. Moved everyone out. Well, you saw. It's been deserted since 1943.'

2

CHRISTMAS AND THE NEW YEAR HAD COME AND gone. The daffodils were just beginning to come out and the first daisies were starting to appear in the grass. Anyone watching from Gibbet Manor would have seen a dark-haired boy in his early teens walking alone across the sloping lawn beside the driveway.

'What do you think of the new kids?' Ben asked the person who wasn't walking beside him.

'Some of them are OK. You're one of the old boys now,' Sam told him.

They crossed the drive, heading round to the side of the house. Ben left faint footmarks on the dew-glistening grass. His sister Sam didn't.

'I still have so much to learn,' Ben said. 'It's like, the more they tell me about ghosts and demons and spirits and Grotesques, I realise the less I actually know. The new kids just get an overview. Then they're off, back to their real schools. But me and Rupam and Gemma and Maria – we're in this so *deep* . . .'

They walked on in silence for several moments. Then Sam said, 'That girl Jenny's a bit weird. She dreams she's her own great-great-grandmother living in Barnsley.'

Ben laughed. 'You're dead – you can talk!'

It had been a shock, of course. When Ben first realised that no one else could see his older sister, that she had died, he'd been devastated. But to him Sam seemed every bit as real and alive as ever. She couldn't remember anything about what had happened to her – the ceremony performed by the devilish Carstairs Endeavour to raise a powerful demon . . . Her *death*.

Sam wasn't with Ben all the time. It seemed to be an effort for her. She came when she could, stayed as long as possible. She never talked about where she went when she was not with him. Maybe she was nowhere, or maybe their time together seemed constant and continuous to Sam, or maybe she was – quite literally – in Hell.

In his quest to learn the truth about what had happened to his sister, Ben had ended up here, at Gibbet Manor, in the middle of Dartmoor. The School of Night, it was called – nicknamed after its founder, Dirk Knight. The children who came here were gifted with the ability to see ghosts and demons, to sense the extraordinary. As far as Knight knew, Ben was one of those children.

But the truth was very different. The only ghost Ben could see without the help of the special mobile phone that all the children had was Sam. He'd bluffed his way into the school. Now he was bluffing in order to stay.

Even so, he was beginning to sense things. There was a sort of stirring somewhere deep inside him, as if he was starting to feel the approach of the supernatural. Not that he'd ever be as gifted as Gemma, one of the few other permanent pupils here. He'd never see as much as Sam had done when she was alive . . . He felt more like Maria – just eighteen and already losing her abilities as she grew into an adult and left the innocent, open-minded state of childhood behind.

Then there was Rupam. He was Ben's best friend, but Ben couldn't pretend he understood the boy. Sometimes Rupam saw the ghosts and spirits, and he knew all there was to know about Indian and Asian creatures and demons. But most impressive was his memory. He had only to hear or read something once and he'd remember it forever.

Show him a photograph for just a minute and weeks later he could describe it in exact detail.

Even the latest intake of new pupils had more ability and talent than Ben. They were already nearing the end of their residential course and would soon be sent home to parents who thought they'd been on an Outward Bound course, camping and enjoying outdoor activities on Dartmoor, with no idea what they'd really been learning about.

Ben hadn't been at the School of Night that long himself. He was used to being moved from foster family to foster family, orphanage to institution – had been for as long as he could recall. He didn't remember either of his parents. But up until now he'd always had his sister with him, looking after him.

It was strange. Ben had never felt more at home than he did at the School of Night. But he had never felt more alone and out of place either.

Just that morning, one of the boys – tall and thin, with dark hair and glasses – had made some sarky comment to Ben about how he knew it all. Ben was painfully aware that he didn't. And he feared that even the new students would soon see he was a fake, that he had no right to be here.

In a school where everyone else could see through the fabric of reality and into the realm of the supernatural, being able to chat to the ghost of your dead sister seemed unimpressive and ordinary.

A raised, paved terrace ran down the side of the house. Stone steps led up to it, but Ben and Sam walked past them. The grounds behind the house were less well cared for, the grass long and the whole area more like moorland and pasture than garden.

The path was really just a track worn through the grass. It wound lazily between the occasional trees and formed a long loop back to the other side of the house. As they reached the furthest point of the loop, a figure stepped out from behind a large copper beech tree.

He was short and stocky, with thinning grey hair that straggled across his balding head. Pendleton Jones looked after the grounds of Gibbet Manor. He laid traps for the smaller demons that crept in over the walls or through the gates. He was holding a spade, and Ben saw a pair of shears and a bucket half full of prunings beside the tree.

'Hello there,' Ben called as he approached.

He liked Jones, who was easy to talk to and down to earth. When he was with him, he didn't feel so much of a fraud, so inadequate.

'Who was that with you?' Jones asked.

Instinctively, Ben turned to look at Sam, but she had gone. He was alone.

'How did you know?' he asked. No one could see Sam – not even Gemma, and she saw *everything*.

Jones shrugged. 'Heard you talking. Don't worry. I talk to myself sometimes. Well, quite often actually. No one else to talk to out here usually.'

'You should come to the house. Let Mrs Bailey give you a cup of tea.'

Jones shook his head. 'They don't want me bothering them. Mrs Bailey's busy enough keeping you kids under control and running the place without making cups of tea for the likes of me. Anyway, I've got my Thermos.' He looked round. 'Somewhere. Must have left it in the shed. Never mind.'

'You busy?' Ben asked.

'Always busy. Spring's coming, so there's lots to do. Plants and trees don't look after themselves.'

They talked for a while. There was a chill breeze blowing across the moor, but the bright sun warmed Ben's face.

'You found out any more about your poor sister?' Jones asked.

They were sitting on the grass, leaning back against the wide trunk of the copper beech.

'Not really,' Ben admitted. 'That page, torn from

22

an old book, which Carstairs Endeavour had . . .'

'I remember.'

Ben had told Jones how, after defeating Endeavour, they had found a photocopied page from an ancient book – one of the artefacts that Gabriel Diablo used to summon the demon Mortagula.

'Knight said he knew that Endeavour didn't have the actual page, only the photocopy. And I know why. He showed me.'

'Showed you?'

'Knight's got the real book and he showed me the page. And on it . . .' Ben shook his head, still unable to understand it. 'On it is a drawing of Sam. It's definitely her. I mean, it's only a drawing, but I know my sister when I see her.'

'And the picture was drawn when?'

'In the seventeenth century. Hundreds of years ago. So how can it show Sam?'

'More to the point,' Jones said, 'how did Endeavour get hold of a copy of a page when Knight keeps the book locked up here safe and sound?'

Ben nodded. He'd wondered exactly the same thing. 'And how many of Diablo's artefacts does Endeavour have? If he gets them all – the two books, the Crystal that focuses his power, the Dagger and the Amulet – he'll try again. He'll raise Mortagula.'

Jones picked up his spade. 'Then you'd better stop him.'

'Got to find him first. There's been no sign of Endeavour since last year. Knight's got everyone keeping a lookout for him. But nothing so far.'

'He'll turn up. Bad things always do.'

Ben nodded. 'That's what worries me,' he said quietly.

Jones didn't hear. He was shading his eyes from the sun with his hand and staring down past the house to the bottom of the drive. A car was coming slowly into the grounds. It stopped and a man got out to close and lock the gates behind him. He was tall and lean, with close-cropped hair, and he was wearing a khaki uniform.

'Captain Morton,' Ben said, recognising him at once.

'If the army's here, maybe a war's about to start.' Jones smiled. 'Or perhaps he's just come for a cup of Mrs Bailey's famous tea.'

'We'd better get back,' Sam said, stepping out from behind the tree.

Jones didn't see her. He waved and returned to his work as Ben took his dead sister's hand and they hurried back along the path to the house.

3

BEN WAS ABOUT TO RING THE BELL WHEN THE front door swung open.

'Mrs Bailey,' Ben said.

'I was in the hall. I . . .' She hesitated. 'Well, I heard you coming.'

Mrs Bailey was in charge of the day-to-day running of the school and also of Dirk Knight's business life. She looked slightly severe as well as professional in her dark trouser suit, with her short ice-blonde hair scraped back. But she was the closest that Ben, or any of his friends, had to a mother. For all that, he knew almost nothing about her – not her first name, not even if there was, or ever had been, a *Mr* Bailey.

'I was coming to find you anyway,' Mrs Bailey went on as she stepped aside to let him into the house. 'Mr Knight has asked if you can join him and the others in the lecture hall.'

'Everyone?' Ben wondered.

'Not all the children. Just Rupam and Gemma. And Maria of course.'

It was only after she'd spoken that Ben realised he hadn't actually asked the question out loud. He'd been about to, but as she often did Mrs Bailey had guessed exactly what was on his mind.

'Is this because Captain Morton is here?' Ben asked.

This time, she didn't answer him before he'd asked the question. She didn't answer him at all.

'Lecture hall – quick as you can. They're waiting for you.'

The room was at the back of the house. It was just like the sort of lecture hall you might find on a university campus. Tiers of fixed fold-down seats looked on to a circular stage. At the moment the lights were low, so Ben stood at the back of the large room letting his eyes adjust to the gloom.

A screen at the back of the stage was showing grainy video footage that Ben knew at once was from a mobile phone like the one he had been given. The phone's camera could detect supernatural or paranormal activity to a far greater degree than all but the most psychic children. The phone also recorded the images and sent them direct to the School of Night for analysis.

Anyone who had psychic ability glowed faintly on the phone's screen. Gemma, the most gifted of them all, shone brightly. Sam – so Knight had once told Ben – had whited out the screen . . . Now, although the screen showed most ghosts and spirits, Sam didn't show at all on Ben's phone.

Ben settled himself down next to where Rupam was sitting. His friend's attention was on the screen, and beyond him Ben could see the dark silhouettes of Gemma and Maria also watching intently. He was vaguely aware of Mrs Bailey taking a seat in one of the other rows, close to a burly figure Ben recognised as the Reverend Alistair Growl, one of the School of Night's teachers.

The images on the screen were shaky pictures of a lane. There wasn't much ambient light and Ben guessed the video had been shot as it was getting dark. It was obviously taken from inside a car – Ben could see the edge of the dashboard, reflections on the windscreen and the side window as the camera-phone moved to catch the figures that were walking past.

Glowing figures. Almost ethereal. Ghosts.

A man in an ill-fitting, tattered sports jacket smiled at the camera. But it was a humourless smile and Ben doubted the man could even see the car as it drove past. Behind the man, a woman carried a small child, blurring and glowing as they walked.

Then the figures were gone. Something else glowed slightly in the distance. A tall building, glimpsed through trees. The screen juddered and went blank.

For a moment the room was in darkness. Out of that darkness, Ben heard Knight's voice.

'There's more in a moment. Once Webby gets his act together . . .'

Webby was the computer expert. The video was automatically downloaded from the phone – any phone supplied by the School of Night – if anything out of the ordinary was detected. Webby, who checked what came in, was now playing it back from one of the huge mainframe computers in the cellars of the house. Cellars that Webby himself never seemed to leave. He even had a bed made up down there.

The screen came back to life. The images were darker now, confused and claustrophobic. They seemed to show close-up views of hedges and trees, bushes and shrubs. It looked as if the car was driving straight at them. The leaves glowed faintly and branches gave off an incandescent glow. But at the same time, Ben realised, he could see *through* the vegetation – he could see a perfectly ordinary roadway curving ahead of the car.

The camera was shuddering, moving back and forth so erratically and quickly that it made Ben feel carsick to watch. Just as he thought he would have to look away, a dark opening appeared in the vegetation. The opening seemed to race towards the car, and suddenly Ben was watching mobile phone video of an open road as the vehicle burst through the hedge.

The screen blanked out again, but almost immediately the image returned. This time it showed a brief shot of a soldier walking towards the car. Behind him were a barrier, a small hut and several vehicles . . .

Then the image disappeared and the lights came up. Ben blinked in the sudden brightness.

'There is sound as well, but it's not very informative,' Knight said, stepping on to the stage.

He was a tall man, wearing a dark business suit and a white shirt with a plain tie. He looked like a civil servant or an off-duty senior police officer. The man who was now standing beside him on the stage, Captain Morton, was also tall and broad. In his army uniform he was a military mirror image of Knight.

'Glad you could join us, Ben,' Knight said.

Before Ben could apologise for being late, he went on, 'That video was from the phone of one of our students, Tommy MacMillan. It was taken when he and his father got lost in Dorset when returning from holiday a few days ago. Tommy subsequently called in, though Webby had already flagged up the footage as being of interest.'

'They'd somehow strayed into a military area,' Captain Morton said. He glanced at Knight, who nodded for him to continue. 'They should have been stopped. There are checkpoints on all the roads in and out. We're not quite sure why they weren't spotted. You just got a glimpse there at the end of Tommy and Mr MacMillan arriving at the wrong side of a checkpoint on their way out.'

Reverend Growl cleared his throat. 'And why is this of interest to us, might I ask? I saw a few ghosts, which didn't seem to be causing anyone any trouble, and a lot of hedgerows. Rather than coming to us, perhaps young Tommy should persuade his father to invest in an advanced driving course?'

Knight smiled. 'A fair point. But the military aspect is worrying. At first I felt the same as you, Alistair. But I asked Morton to make a few enquiries and . . .' He turned to Morton. 'Well, you can tell everyone.'

'As you've surmised, there doesn't appear to be any immediate threat, though young Tommy was a bit shaken up. But Templeton is right in the middle of an army training area.'

'Templeton?' Rupam put his hand up. 'That's one of those villages that was evacuated during the Second World War, isn't it?'

'Correct, young man. It was in 1943, when the Allies were already planning for the D-Day invasion of Normandy. They took over several villages in Dorset, among other places. Best known is Tyneham, but also Turelhampton and Templeton. Places beginning with "T" in fact, though I don't think that's significant.' He smiled to show it was a joke.

A few seats along from Ben, Maria laughed. She was leaning forward, hanging on his every word. She ran a hand through her long, curly dark hair. Her usual sulky expression had been replaced by one of interest and enthusiasm. Ben nudged Rupam and they both grinned. The older girl's admiration for Captain Morton was barely disguised at the best of times.

'So,' Morton went on, 'in 1943 everyone was moved out. They were rehoused like evacuees, which I suppose they were, and told they could return home after the war. Except it never happened. The War Office and later the Ministry of Defence kept the area for training all through the Cold War. Most of the other ghost villages – as they are rather aptly called – are now open to the public at certain times. But Templeton is still right in the thick of things. Strictly off limits.'

'And haunted,' Gemma pointed out.

'Not until now, so far as we know,' Knight said. 'But yes, haunted. The village has been dead and deserted for nearly seventy years. Now it's coming back to life. Mr MacMillan and his son spoke to villagers, even had a drink in the pub.'

'Do we have any satellite information?' Mrs Bailey asked.

Morton shook his head. 'Restricted area. Off limits. There are ways of preventing any observation, which I'm not allowed to mention. If you look at Google Earth or something like that, you'll find images of other parts of Dorset. It's a good match, but it isn't what's actually there.'

'The army's rather touchy about it all,' Knight explained. 'They won't even let us see the relevant documents dating back to the evacuation order, or the parish records.'

'The key to this may very well be in the history

of the village,' Growl pointed out. 'Seeing those records could be vital if we're to lay these poor souls to rest and discover what's happening here.'

'I agree,' Knight said. 'And I've made certain arrangements which I hope will provide the information we need despite what the Ministry of Defence tells us.'

Ben nudged Rupam again, wondering if he knew what Knight meant. But Rupam just shrugged.

'So what do we do?' Maria asked. 'Go in and exorcise the ghosts so the army can get back to playing soldiers there without the poor squaddies getting spooked?'

'Perhaps. But, as the Reverend says, we need to understand what's happening. This may indeed be a simple case of exorcism, but remember, these ghosts are powerful and substantial enough for even adults to see them clearly. So it may be that what is happening in Templeton is growing stronger and is a symptom of something more widespread and dangerous. We need to find out. But there is another slight problem we need to address first.'

Growl gave a chuckle. 'You mean a slight problem other than ghosts returning to the village they were forcibly evacuated from in life and selling tourists pints of beer, somehow allowing civilians into a restricted military zone, and the MOD refusing to let us see any relevant paperwork?'

'Colonel Oliver Greene,' Knight said.

'He's the officer in charge of the facility that centres on Templeton,' Morton explained. 'We've shut down his training ground while we investigate. On the one hand, he wants his village back and the training of his units to continue as planned as soon as possible. On the other hand, he thinks this whole ghost thing is a lot of nonsense made up by a couple of tourists who were somewhere they shouldn't have been. He thinks they're making it up to get out of trouble, and that other sightings are just hoaxes or hysteria.'

'In short, he's hardly taking the matter seriously.'

'Then Captain Morton should go and see him,' Mrs Bailey suggested.

'I'd rather keep a low profile,' Morton said. 'He outranks me. I don't want to intimidate him or upset him into ordering me about if I can avoid it.'

'Plus, very few people know about Captain Morton's liaison role with us,' Knight added. 'I'd like to keep it that way. Greene doesn't know and doesn't need to know. Not yet, anyway. Which is why *I'm* going to see him. Tomorrow.'

'Do you need moral support?' Growl offered.

'Just Gemma, if you don't mind.'

'This guy's an army officer,' Maria said. 'You need to impress him. You should take someone else as well.'

'Feeling left out again?' Rupam murmured.

Ben didn't think he had intended Maria to hear, but she glared at him.

'I suppose that's a fair point,' Knight said. 'All right, yes.'

Maria smiled in satisfaction and glanced again at Rupam. But her triumph was short-lived.

Because Knight said, 'Ben, you'll come with us. We can squeeze you in the back of the Morgan. Straight after breakfast, please. Make sure you look presentable.'

The clock by his bed said it was two in the morning. Ben didn't know what had woken him, but he was instantly awake.

'Did you hear something?' Sam was standing at the closed door, listening. 'There it is again.'

Ben struggled out from under his duvet. It had become wrapped round his legs in a tangle. 'Don't I get any time off?' he grumbled.

'From the school or from me?' She didn't expect an answer. 'Come on, let's see what it is.'

The sound was louder when Ben opened the door. Metallic. A clanking noise from downstairs. He tiptoed into the corridor and along to the landing.

'Don't say anything,' Sam said. 'They might hear you.' She spoke in a whisper, even though nobody would be able to hear *her*.

Someone was in the hall. A dark figure, dressed entirely in black. Ben looked down between the banisters on the stairs, keeping out of sight as he watched. Whoever it was had knelt on the floor, facing away, their upper body in shadow. There was a large leather bag open at their feet. The metallic clanking sound came from inside as they rummaged round and rearranged the contents of the bag. The faint light gleamed on metal tools . . .

It was a woman. The black bodysuit emphasised her figure as she closed the bag and stood up. Ben couldn't see her face, but he knew who it was immediately from the collar-length white-blonde hair.

Mrs Bailey let herself out of the house, closing the front door quietly behind her. A few moments later, Ben heard the sound of a car crunching on the gravel forecourt.

'What's she doing?' he wondered out loud.

But there was no one else there to hear him.

4

THEY WAITED FOR OVER HALF AN HOUR IN THE canteen at the army base. Soldiers came and went. Most of them ignored Ben, Gemma and Knight. But some stared openly at them, obviously wondering who they were.

One woman in khaki uniform came over and asked them if she could help.

'We're waiting for Colonel Greene,' Knight told her. 'He knows we're here, but thanks for asking.'

'You might have a long wait,' the woman confided. 'The colonel doesn't hurry to keep appointments with people he doesn't want to see.'

'How do you know he doesn't want to see us?' Ben asked.

'Because he didn't invite us to wait outside his office,' Knight said. 'Am I right?' he asked the woman soldier.

'Not for me to say, sir.' Her smile said it clearly enough. 'They'll give you coffee if you ask.'

Gemma and Ben chatted quietly. Knight sat in absolute silence, his eyes focused on nothing. Thinking.

Finally, it seemed that Greene was ready to see them. A young soldier marched purposefully across the canteen straight towards them.

'Call my mobile,' Knight said quietly to Gemma. 'Don't let him see you do it.'

The soldier stopped in front of the table where they were sitting. Gemma turned away, thumbing her mobile.

'Mr Knight? The colonel is ready to see you now.'

'So soon?' Knight yawned, stretched and stood up. Then his mobile rang. 'Excuse me.' He took out his phone and checked the display, angling it away from the soldier. Beside him, Ben could see the word 'Gemma'.

'The colonel is waiting, sir,' the soldier said with evident impatience.

Knight flipped open his phone. 'Sorry, I have to take this. It's the Secretary of State. I imagine he wants to know how we're getting on.' He covered the end of the phone with his hand. 'We'll find our own way. Tell Colonel Greene we'll be along as soon as we can. You know how these politicians like to talk.'

Turning away, Knight lifted the phone to his ear. 'They really don't care who they keep waiting,' he said. Then his tone changed to a hearty greeting: 'Jeremy, how good of you to call . . . No, we haven't yet. The colonel is very busy . . . apparently.'

Knight glanced back to see the soldier marching stiffly away again. 'Priorities, yes, I'll be sure to mention that,' he said loudly, before closing the phone and slipping it back into his pocket. He smiled at Gemma and Ben. 'We'll let the colonel wait for a bit, shall we? See how he likes it.'

After ten minutes, Knight decided they'd let Colonel Greene wait long enough. He accosted a private who led them to the colonel's office. The soldier who'd come to get them was sitting at a desk in a small office outside. He glared at Knight and dismissed the private with a growl of reluctant thanks.

'So many dead people,' Gemma whispered to Ben as they waited again. 'Even in the canteen. Can you feel it?'

Ben shivered. 'No,' he whispered back. 'Well, maybe.'

The door to Greene's office flew open to reveal the colonel standing in the doorway. He was so broad his shoulders almost touched the sides. His hair was cut close to his scalp and his huge hands were clenched into impatient fists.

'Are you Knight?' he demanded. 'You've got twenty minutes.'

'Thank you, Colonel.' Knight followed Greene into the inner office, gesturing for Gemma and Ben to follow. 'But I doubt if that's going to be long enough.'

'Long enough for me to tell you this is all baloney,' Greene retorted. He sat behind his desk and gestured for Knight to take the seat on the other side. 'You brought your family?' he said, nodding at Ben and Gemma, who had taken chairs at the side of the office.

'Colleagues. We recruit them young.'

Greene frowned but made no comment. 'You have friends in important places, Mr Knight,' he said, angling himself so he was obviously ignoring Ben and Gemma. 'My superiors tell me that Templeton is off limits. They tell me that even more important people in government have told them that no one goes into the village until *you* say so.'

'If that's what they tell you, it must be true.'

'Because of a few spooks? I don't buy that. My men aren't scared of ghosts. They don't run from shadows, or believe everything some halfwit tourist who got himself lost tells them. If my men go into that village, what's the worst that can happen to them?'

He leaned back in his chair, smiling thinly as he waited for Knight's reply.

'Tell him, Gemma,' Knight said quietly.

Gemma's chair was so high her feet didn't reach the floor. She kicked her legs as she spoke, her girlish attitude at odds with what she said.

'They might see ghosts. Apparitions. Demons. But that isn't a problem. People see them all the time. Usually kids. Probably the younger soldiers . . . Maybe the ghosts will see them. Maybe they'll come after your soldiers. Maybe they'll put ideas and thoughts in their heads, drive them crazy.' She sniffed. 'Perhaps they'll make them forget who they are or why they're there. Make them get lost, or have fits, or shoot each other.'

The colour was slowly draining from Colonel Greene's face. He opened his mouth to say something, but Gemma hadn't finished.

'Probably we'll never know. You'll just find the bodies. Or more likely you won't find anything at all. They'll just disappear. Like ghosts. It happens. They might end up back in 1943, or they might fall through the same crack in reality all the way to Hell.'

There was silence for several seconds. Then Greene laughed. 'You expect me to believe that childish rubbish?'

'I expect you to obey your orders and keep away from the village until my team have inspected it and declared it safe,' Knight said. He made a point of looking at his watch. 'Actually you were right. It didn't take that long, did it?' He stood up.

'Wait,' Colonel Greene barked. 'I'm not closing down important training and manoeuvres just on the say-so of some suit and a couple of kids.'

Knight sat down again. 'There again . . .' he murmured.

'I got my orders last night, when they told me you jokers were coming. But I'd already sent a patrol into Templeton to check out what that crazy tourist and his son said.' He leaned forward and pressed an intercom button. 'Jenkins, has Corporal Rutherford reported back yet?'

The reply was distorted by the speakers, but it was clear enough. 'Just a couple of minutes ago, sir.'

'Have him report to me here at once.' Greene turned back to Knight. 'We'll soon find out if there's anything weird going on in that village, Mr Knight.

And since I spent a few nights of a training exercise sleeping in the churchyard there just the other week, you can take it from me – there isn't.'

Corporal Rutherford's uniform was spattered with mud and one sleeve was ripped. His face was scratched and dirty, with a couple of days' stubble on his chin. He marched up to the space beside Knight in front of Colonel Greene's desk and saluted smartly.

'At ease,' Greene said.

'Sir.' Rutherford visibly relaxed.

'You and your team were in Templeton for a while, Corporal. These people are keen to know if you witnessed anything unusual.'

Rutherford shook his head. 'All seemed normal. Quiet of course. You'd expect that under the circumstances.'

Knight leaned forward. 'How did you hurt your face?'

Rutherford's hand went instinctively to his cheek. 'Just a scratch, sir. Had a fight with a bramble.' He grinned. 'Most eventful thing that happened, actually.'

Ben glanced at Gemma. She was frowning. Something was wrong. She caught Ben's eye and

shrugged. Something, only she didn't know what
. . . Ben eased his mobile phone out of his pocket
and flipped it open. But there was nothing unusual
about the image of the corporal on the screen.

'Satisfied?' Greene demanded of Knight. Then
he spoke curtly to Rutherford. 'Dismissed. And let
me have a full report soon as you can.'

'Sir.'

Rutherford turned to go. As he did, he saw Ben
holding up his phone. 'What the hell is that?'

'Sorry.' Ben quickly closed the phone and put it
away. 'Sorry. I was just . . .' His voice tailed off as
Knight held up his hand.

'You object to being photographed?' he asked
Rutherford.

The soldier looked at Greene, who remained
impassive. 'No problem, sir. Is that – can I ask? – is
that a camera, then? Must be new. For spies and
agents, is it? SOE?'

'SOE?' Greene echoed. He was frowning now
too.

'Special Operations Executive,' Knight said
quietly. 'They trained and ran agents during the
Second World War.'

'I know,' Greene barked. 'You being funny,
Rutherford?'

'Sir?' He seemed genuinely surprised at Greene's anger.

'Get out!'

'No, wait.' Knight's voice was full of authority, making Rutherford freeze. Knight was holding his own mobile phone – almost identical to Ben's. 'You don't know what this is, do you?'

Greene stood up and walked slowly to the window, staring out across the base towards the woodland beyond. 'Answer Mr Knight's questions, soldier,' he said. Ben could hear the tension in his voice.

'It's a camera, sir. You just said.'

'I said it takes photographs. But it's actually a mobile phone, isn't it?'

Rutherford's astonishment was obvious. 'A *phone*, sir? But it's so small. There's no connection – no wire. Like an RT, is it?'

'A bit like a radio telephone, yes. Now tell me, where have you been for the last twenty-four hours or so?'

'On duty in the village of Templeton, sir.'

'Doing what?'

Rutherford looked to Greene, who turned from the window and nodded. 'Checking everything was all right. That's it really, sir. The village has been evacuated, there's no one there now. All quiet and normal, like I said, sir.'

'You see?' Greene said. 'Exactly as I told you.'

'It's a funny way of saying it, though,' Ben said. He hadn't meant to speak out loud, but he'd been struck by Corporal Rutherford's words.

'Go on,' Knight prompted.

Ben swallowed. 'Well, just the way he said it. "The village has been evacuated" – like it only just happened.'

'And when did it happen?' Knight asked Corporal Rutherford. 'When exactly was the village evacuated?'

'On 27 February 1943. The village of Templeton was evacuated and handed over to the War Office for training and manoeuvres.'

'Satisfied?' Greene asked.

'Your man is very well informed,' Knight said. 'He even knows the exact date of the evacuation. Which is more than I did.'

'Of course, sir,' Rutherford told them. He gave a short, nervous laugh. 'I mean, it was only a couple of weeks ago.'

There was silence. Greene's mouth had dropped open. Gemma stopped swinging her legs. Knight nodded.

Embarrassed at the silence, Rutherford went on,

'The village is empty and quiet, sir. Ready for our lads to start training properly. And now the Yanks are getting properly involved, we can really stick it to Jerry, like Mr Churchill says.'

Knight stood up. 'Thank you, Corporal Rutherford. That's very helpful.' He turned to Greene, who was looking pale. 'I suggest you give this man and the rest of his patrol a complete medical.'

'They'll probably be fine after a good night's sleep,' Gemma said. 'So long as they stay away from the village.'

'But keep an eye on them anyway,' Knight added. 'And as I told you before, I want that village cordoned off, completely out of bounds until my team has been in and inspected it.'

Knight strode across the room, with Gemma and Ben following close behind. He paused as he pulled open the door and turned back towards Greene.

'Unless you still want to argue that there's nothing weird going on?' He barely paused for a reply. 'I thought not. We'll see ourselves out.'

47

5

BEN WAS LIVID.

'There's no point arguing with him,' Sam whispered.

Ben hadn't realised she was there. His anger and frustration were focused on Knight. They were standing on the steps that led up to the front door of Gibbet Manor.

'You are staying here and that's final,' Knight told him. 'I need Gemma, but for this someone with more experience is essential.'

Maria was already getting into the car – not Knight's Morgan but a large hatchback. She gave Ben a sympathetic smile, but he wasn't in the mood to appreciate it.

'After all that stuff with Colonel Greene, I want to see the village.'

'Maybe you will,' Knight told him. 'But not just yet. Besides, I need you here. I need you and Rupam to find out everything you can about Templeton.

Its history, parish records, local stories, the families who lived there – everything.'

'I thought all that was classified,' Ben grumbled.

'Talk to Mrs Bailey. I asked her to see what she could dig up. And get Webby to search the Internet – public access sites and the restricted ones too. There must be something.'

Reverend Growl pushed past them. 'I'm hoping there will be some records remaining in the church,' he said. 'I see that there's a village school as well, which might have kept registers or local documents. From what little we do know, everyone cleared out in rather a hurry. Maybe they left a few clues behind.' He rubbed his hands together enthusiastically. 'Can't wait to get started.'

Ben watched the car pull away. Gemma gave Ben a wave, but Maria, Growl and Knight ignored him.

'No use standing here sulking,' Sam said. 'Why don't you find Rupam and make a start on this research?'

'Rupam's probably memorised it all by now.'

'Probably,' Sam agreed. 'But he needs you to help him understand what it all means. You're the one who can work things through, see the connections, make the links.'

'You think so?'

'Course I do. And so does Knight. That's why he's asked you to do it.'

'He just wants to keep me busy.'

Sam shook her head. 'He doesn't need to do that. There are plenty of other children here just carrying on with their classes. He could have sent you back to school. Instead he's given you a job to do. So stop moping about and do it.'

'I still wish I was going with them,' Ben said, staring down the drive. The car was passing through the gates and disappearing out of sight.

Sam laughed. 'A haunted village? I bet they'll have a really boring time. Probably won't even see that many ghosts.'

'And how many will *I* see, stuck here?' Ben turned to go inside.

'Let's not get personal,' Sam told him.

Gemma felt like a schoolgirl. Knight had told them all to dress in neutral clothes that would not have been too out of place in 1943, so she was in dark trousers and a plain white blouse. Knight had frowned at her trainers but said nothing, so she kept them on.

The only consolation was that Maria looked just as uncomfortable in similar attire. 'It's all right for the men,' she told Gemma in the back of the car.

Knight was in one of his usual dark suits, while Growl was in his black cassock complete with clerical collar.

It took a couple of hours to reach the army checkpoint on the road into Templeton. Knight had a printed pass that Colonel Greene had given him, but the soldiers at the checkpoint were expecting them anyway.

'No one else is to come through, is that clear?' Knight told the soldier in charge.

'Clear as a bell, sir. Colonel Greene's already made that quite plain. No one in or out till this is sorted, unless they have his personal permission.'

'How far is it to the village from here?' Growl asked, leaning across.

'Four miles, near enough.'

Growl nodded. 'Just the distance for a brisk walk in the spring sunshine, don't you think?'

'A walk?' Gemma said.

'Four miles?' Maria added. 'You've got to be kidding!'

'I don't want to take anything into Templeton that isn't from the right time period, when the village was evacuated,' Knight said. 'Growl's correct. We'll

get a bit closer, though, and then leave the car.'
He turned in his seat to look at Maria. 'You're not
wearing high heels, I hope?'

'What if I am?'

'Bad luck.'

'Good job I'm not, then.'

Only Knight was oblivious to the ghosts. He could
have watched them on the screen of his mobile
phone, but for the moment he seemed to have
chosen not to.

Growl could sense them – Gemma knew that
from the way he became quiet and surly. His usual
avuncular character was hidden as he grew more
businesslike and serious. If – when – they came
across stronger spirits than those walking silently
along the lane out of the village, Growl's temper
would flare and at moments like those it was best
to avoid him.

Maria could see them, of course. But Gemma
guessed that the pale, ethereal figures she herself saw
were even less substantial to Maria. She was eighteen
now and with every passing month the older girl's
powers seemed to fade further . . . Gemma looked
forward to the day when she didn't see the ghosts
any more, but it seemed to scare Maria.

'Ah, the church,' Growl announced.

The tower was visible between the trees. The top was ragged and the roof was missing. It looked as if a giant had bitten it off, leaving the uneven remains sticking up like a broken tooth into the sky.

'I did manage to do a little research into the parish,' Growl admitted. 'There are mentions of the church in some of the architectural texts. It's unusual in that the tower is separate from the main building.'

'Why did they build it like that?' Maria wondered.

'If I knew, I'd have told you, wouldn't I?' Growl snapped. Immediately, he apologised. 'Sorry, the texts didn't give a reason. Probably some local legend or story – there usually is in such cases. I hope we'll find some clue in the church itself.'

'It may not matter,' Knight said. 'The church is old.'

'Fourteenth century,' Growl agreed.

Knight thought for a moment, then said, 'What's happening here only started in the last month. Something has changed recently. So looking at old records and documents might not help us at all.'

'Or it might be something that happened in 1943, but it's only having an effect now,' Gemma suggested. 'All these people had to leave home. That's so sad.'

'Upheaval, trauma, resentment,' Knight agreed. 'Bound to disturb the place. Good point, Gemma. But I think there must be a more recent trigger, even if the underlying problem is from back in 1943.'

'All these people . . .' Maria gestured to ghosts that only she and Gemma could actually see. 'Gemma's right. It was traumatic. Devastating. It changed their lives out of all recognition in a single day. A whole village, a whole community just . . . stopped.'

Knight had his mobile out and was watching on the screen now. 'Yes. But I don't think they're important. They're just echoes, playing out the same day over and over again. Endlessly leaving the village.'

'What about the pub where our friend Tommy got his lemonade?' Growl said. 'There was interaction there, not just a replay of past events.'

'But to no purpose, or no purpose that we know of. Though maybe the pub is the place to start.'

'Tommy's dad saw the ghosts in the pub,' Maria told Knight. 'Maybe you will too.'

'There's something to look forward to,' Knight said. He didn't sound convinced.

The ghosts had stopped their ethereal evacuation by the time Gemma and the others reached the welcome sign with the name of the village painted out.

'They did that at the start of the war,' Knight explained. 'They took down or blotted out any signs that might help the Germans if they invaded.'

'Not much fear of an invasion by 1943,' Growl said. 'Hitler had made the mistake of attacking Russia and the Americans had joined in the war in Europe.'

'Perhaps they just didn't like strangers,' Maria said.

The lane opened out as they entered the village. There was a row of houses down one side. They looked ready to collapse – roofless shells, their empty window frames rotting away. The lane branched off, leading to more houses one way, the church and the school the other. An old-fashioned street lamp stood at the fork in the road.

The pub was opposite the first row of houses. Its sign was gone, leaving an empty metal frame that creaked in the breeze.

'The Green Man,' Knight said. 'According to Tommy.'

'Whatever,' Maria sniffed. 'Doesn't look like it's open anyway.'

Gemma stared round. She couldn't see anyone any more. No ghosts, no echoes of the past at all.

Except . . . 'The church,' she murmured. 'There's something about the church.'

'The whole place is a ruin,' Growl pointed out. 'Not just the church. The houses have lost their windows and roofs. Falling down. The ghosts can have it.'

'What's that little hut?' Gemma wondered, pointing to what looked like a tall, thin shed with broken windows round the top.

'Phone box,' Knight said, sparing it a glance. 'We'll look inside the pub anyway. You might pick up something.'

The pub was empty. Dust and rubble were strewn over the flagged floor. A few broken struts remained across the roof – visible through a hole in the ceiling and the collapsed upper floor. A round table stood lopsided in the corner, with several chairs lying in pieces beside it.

Broken glass crunched under Gemma's feet as she walked behind the bar. There were a few dusty bottles lying on their sides. One of the beer pump handles was snapped off and another was completely missing.

'I'm getting nothing,' Maria said, looking round with obvious distaste. 'Nothing useful anyway.'

'Gemma?' Knight asked.

She could feel something, but nothing significant. 'Maria's right. There are echoes and ghosts, but no more than anywhere else. Nothing unusual.'

The ghosts of the past were all around her. If she focused, concentrated, she could see them: the old men playing dominoes, the barmaid wiping the glasses. She instinctively knew who they were, and something of their background and history. She watched Henry Jones slapping his son for being stupid. Davie Moorhouse, who slipped and fell in 1876 and banged his head and never got up again, was lying on the floor in a pool of spilt beer and spreading blood . . .

'Poor man,' Gemma said quietly.

'He was drunk,' Maria said, seeing where Gemma was looking. But there was a sadness in her eyes too.

'There's no point in staying here,' Growl decided, leading the way back to the door.

There was an old woman standing in the doorway. Gemma could tell from their reactions that Growl and Knight could see her too. But she wasn't *real*. She had white hair tied back with a black ribbon and was leaning heavily on a walking stick that looked as if it was made from a gnarled branch of an ancient tree.

Her voice was as old and cracked as her wrinkled face. 'Beware the green.'

'I beg your pardon,' Growl said.

'The green. You watch out, clergyman. And the rest of you.' She nodded emphatically, then turned to go.

Growl and Knight exchanged looks before hurrying after her.

Gemma and Maria were close behind. But suddenly all they could see were two men standing outside the pub in the midday sunshine. Alone in an empty, deserted village.

6

MARIA LOOKED ALL ROUND. SHE DIDN'T WANT to check her phone. What if she was the only one who couldn't see the woman now? What if even Knight had more 'sight' than she did – what use would she be then?

Gemma was close beside her. Maria liked Gemma – the girl reminded her so much of herself when she was that age and had first worked for Knight. But at the same time her presence was a constant reminder that Maria was getting older, that her powers were fading . . . that she was being replaced.

'She's gone,' Gemma said quietly.

'Yes,' Maria said. 'I can see that.'

'I'm assuming she was a ghost,' Knight said.

'What did she mean, I wonder?' Growl mused, tapping his chin with a thoughtful finger. '*Beware the green* – the pub, perhaps? The Green Man?'

'The village green,' Knight suggested. 'Though I don't see one.'

'It's quiet again,' Gemma said. 'The woman's gone and all the ghosts have left.'

'Even the birds have stopped,' Maria realised.

Knight had his phone out again. 'No signal. Typical.'

'We received young Tommy's information,' Growl said.

'It would have been sent when the phone got a signal again,' Knight told him. 'No one lives here. The army has its own communications. I'm not surprised the mobiles can't connect.'

'Makes it difficult to find out how Webby and the others are doing with their research,' Maria said.

'Let's try the church,' Knight decided. 'Then I'll go and get the car. I'm sure we had a signal outside the village. I'll drive back and call from the checkpoint on the road if necessary.'

'You don't think the car will put off our spooky friends?' Growl asked.

'They're not doing much for us now,' Maria told him.

'Tommy's dad was driving a modern car,' Gemma said. 'And they saw more than we have.'

'There must be a way to trigger it,' Maria said thoughtfully.

'It was worth a try, fitting in as best we could

with 1943, but there's equipment in the car . . . things we'll need. And I'd like to be able to leave in a hurry if we need to,' Knight said. 'Still, we'll look at the church first.'

Maria kept her eyes focused on the church doors. All through the graveyard she looked neither left nor right. She knew what she would see. Sometimes she wished her powers would fade more quickly. But then she realised that would simply mean she couldn't see what was really happening all round her. She knew how Knight must feel – knowing he couldn't see whether demons were creeping up on him, possibly about to attack.

The church was in a similar state to the pub. A rat scurried away when Knight pushed open what was left of the door. The wooden pews were rotting and the floor was scattered with plaster and stone. A grinning gargoyle from the roof lay on its broken back and stared up at Maria as she followed Growl along the nave.

'It's like the pub,' Gemma said.

'There are echoes and ghosts from the past,' Maria agreed. 'But nothing that's unusual for a church.'

'If there are any records, they will likely be in the vestry,' Growl said.

On the wall above a huge archway there was a painting. It was faded, the paint peeling away and the plaster turning to powder. All Maria could see was a confused mess of figures apparently lying in heaps. A river snaked between them. Flaking angels looked down from above. A devil with a pitchfork had lost half its face and one of its horns.

'What is it?' Gemma asked, following Maria's gaze.

'A doom painting,' Growl said, looking up. 'Probably very fine in its day. It shows the Last Judgement. Demons and angels separating the wheat from the chaff, the Christians from the sinners.'

Maria found it more unsettling than the ghosts she had seen in the pub. She quickly followed Growl and Knight.

The roof of the vestry was still in place and it seemed like a room in a different building. Everything was layered in dust and cobwebs hung from the window and walls, but the structure seemed intact.

A plain, dark wooden desk stood against a wall with an upright chair beside it. The whitewash on the wall above was peeling away in large sheets like paper. Flakes of white were scattered across the desktop and the floor. The tattered remains of a curtain hung from a tarnished rail across an alcove. Behind it, several cassocks and surplices were rotting.

'The choir has long since stopped singing,' Growl said quietly as he examined them.

There was a safe in the corner of the room. The door was ajar and Maria pulled it open. She stood back to let them all see that it was empty.

Gemma was checking the drawers of the desk. The first was empty. The next contained a pile of leather-bound books.

'Parish registers,' Growl exclaimed as Gemma lifted the books out and put them on the desk. He rubbed his hands together. 'Old and fragile, but mercifully not too damp. Now we're getting somewhere. Anything else, my girl?'

In the last drawer was another book. It was less impressive than the registers – little more than a notebook with a stiff cardboard cover. Gemma opened it.

'Parishioners of Templeton – February 1943,' she read out loud.

She turned the page. There was a simple list of names down one side, written in bold capital letters. Against each was a neat address, followed by a signature. Some of the names had been signed simply with an 'X'.

'All the villagers who were evacuated,' Knight said as he looked over Gemma's shoulder.

'Why the X?' Maria asked. 'Did they die or something?'

'Either they couldn't write or they were too young to sign for themselves, I imagine,' Growl told her.

'The names don't seem to be in any order,' Maria noticed. 'They're not alphabetical. Just in families.'

'Most important first, perhaps?' Knight suggested.

'Maybe they just signed when they turned up to church,' Gemma said. 'The vicar signed first. Look. Reverend Josiah Oaken.'

'Rector, more likely,' Growl said. 'Anne Oaken must be his wife. Then his son probably – James Oaken.' He leafed through the book, reading off some of the names. 'Jack Willow, Matthew Pine, Emily Heather . . .' Growl clicked his tongue thoughtfully. 'That's interesting.'

'What?' Knight asked.

'So many of these names are trees or plants. Anthony Beech, Belinda Appleseed, Marcus Wood . . . Coincidence or history, I wonder?'

'Derived from a few common roots, maybe? If you'll forgive the pun,' Knight said.

'Could be, could be.' Growl dusted off the chair beside the desk and sat down. 'Now this will be invaluable if I am to build up a picture of life in the village before it was evacuated. We know who was here. The registers can give us dates of birth, or at least christening, as well as any recent deaths, marriages and so on. I might even be able to identify the people Tommy and his father saw. Gemma, you can help by reading out the names in the registers, then I'll cross-reference them with this list of the parishioners in 1943.'

'We'll fetch the car,' Knight said to Maria. 'At least then we can start getting a bit more scientific.'

'What did you bring?' Maria asked as they left the vestry.

Knight's answer echoed in the empty church: 'The usual stuff. Digital video and sound recorders, thermometers, motion detectors . . .'

She didn't fancy the walk back to the car. But it had to be better than looking through dusty old books with Growl, Maria thought. Gemma was going to be so bored.

The high hedges along the side of the narrow road made it difficult to judge how far they had come. But they had long since passed the painted-out village sign.

'Can't be far now to the car,' Knight said. 'If we

get to the checkpoint we know we've gone too far.'

Maria didn't reply. She was bored and it was starting to rain. She wondered whether Gemma would be able to see the ghosts still leaving the village, walking with them along the road. Would she herself have seen them a year ago? A month ago? Had she lost the ability in the hour since they arrived?

She was tempted to get out her phone and see if the ghosts were there. But she couldn't bear the thought of Knight knowing how weak she'd become. She couldn't bear her own inadequacy.

The road curved, rising gently. Round the hedge, Maria at last saw the checkpoint – the wooden barrier lowered across the road.

'Strange. We must have passed the turn-off where we left the car,' Knight said.

'I didn't see it,' Maria said.

There were two soldiers standing at the end of the barrier. They turned as they saw Knight and Maria approaching. One of them slipped his rifle off his shoulder and took aim.

Maria skidded to a halt. She recognised them – both the soldiers had been there when they arrived. She could see Knight's car pulled in off the road beyond the barrier.

'Careful,' Knight said quietly, his hand on Maria's shoulder. 'I don't like this.'

'Who are you?' the soldier shouted. 'State your business and show us authorisation or I'll fire.'

'You can't just shoot people,' Maria yelled back.

'It's all right,' Knight called. He walked slowly towards the barrier. 'You remember us. We came through earlier. I have authorisation from Colonel Greene.'

'Never heard of him,' the other soldier said. He had his rifle levelled at them now. 'And we ain't never seen you two before neither.'

Knight stopped. 'What's the date?' he asked.

'You what?'

The two soldiers glanced at each other.

'It's a simple enough question,' Knight said, backing away slowly.

Maria had a bad feeling about all this. She flipped open her phone, but it showed nothing unusual. And it still wasn't getting a signal.

'Stop right there,' the closer of the two soldiers said. 'You put your hands up and walk slowly towards us, right?'

'Oh, don't be stupid,' Maria said. 'You know who we are.'

'You could be anyone,' the other soldier said.

'You're in a restricted area without permission. Spies, that's what you are.'

'And we shoot spies,' the first solider added.

'You can't shoot us,' Maria said again. She was backing away now too.

The soldier gave a short laugh. 'Don't you know there's a war on?'

'All right, all right,' Knight said quickly. 'We'll cooperate.' He turned slowly towards Maria, his hands in the air. 'Won't we, Maria.' Facing away from the soldiers, he mouthed, 'Run!'

Maria smiled. 'Of course we will.'

Then she turned and ran. She was aware of Knight close behind her. There was a crack like a branch breaking. Then another. But it was only when a bullet thumped into the road just in front of her that Maria realised the soldiers were firing at them.

'They think it's 1943,' Knight gasped as he caught her up.

'They're not ghosts. And those bullets are real.'

'Just like Corporal Rutherford. We can't get out of the village that way.'

They slowed to a brisk walk.

'Are they following?' Maria asked.

'Manning the checkpoint. They know we can't get out.'

'Because there are checkpoints on all the roads?'

Knight nodded. 'Sooner or later we'll meet soldiers. I wonder how far the effect extends. Too far, I suspect. We'll have to try cross-country.'

'Got to find a way through the hedge first,' Maria pointed out. 'There must be a field or something on the other side.' She chose a point where the hedge looked less dense and tried to force the branches apart. 'I can't see through,' she said after a while. 'It seems to go on forever.'

There seemed to be a gate further along, close to the village sign, so they made their way towards it.

When they got there, they found the gate didn't open into a field or on to a track. Instead, immediately behind it there was a mass of shrubs and greenery, as if the hedge had grown along behind it.

'I thought it was open country through there,' Maria said.

'So did I.' Knight checked his phone again. 'Still no signal. And now no way out. You know, I don't think we're supposed to leave this village.'

'Why can't we get out? Are we trapped?' Maria felt a wave of panic sweep over her. She still hadn't caught her breath after running from the soldiers and now she was hemmed in by hedges. Even the sky seemed darker and lower.

'We have to find out what's going on – what's causing all this to happen, and to happen now.'

'Then we can stop it and leave,' Maria added.

'But we're going to need the information Ben and Rupam get from Webby and Mrs Bailey.'

Maria sighed. 'No way. We haven't got a signal and we can't find a way out. I don't suppose you're going to tell me that the phone box in the village is still connected.' She felt for a moment as if she wanted just to sit down in the middle of the road and cry. 'We could be stuck here for *days* before anyone realises there's a problem and comes looking for us.'

'It's worse than that.' Knight's face fell into shadow as he stared across at the church tower rising above the hedges in the distance. It was no longer a broken ruin. Now it was complete again. 'Look. To some extent the whole village has slipped back to 1943, just after it was evacuated. First Tommy and his dad saw the village before the people left. We saw them leaving. And now this . . .'

Maria felt herself go cold as she began to take in the implications. 'Just what are you saying?'

Knight turned back to Maria. 'I'm saying that it could be nearly seventy years before anyone realises there's a problem and comes looking for us.'

The sound of the doorbell reached Ben and Rupam in the large library of Gibbet Manor.

They were working their way through a heap of reference books and a pile of papers and documents that Mrs Bailey had provided – with no explanation of where they had come from. There were electoral lists, copies of the letter sent to every resident of Templeton and the posters that had been put up, even minutes of a Cabinet meeting at which the evacuation had been agreed . . .

'Wonder who that is at the door?' Ben said.

He was making notes on a large pad of lined paper, though he wasn't sure how useful they would be to Growl or anyone else.

Rupam was at the window. 'It's a police car.'

Moments later, the door opened and Mrs Bailey led in a man in a crumpled dark suit. He was carrying a metal briefcase.

'Ben Foundling?' the man asked.

Was this it? Had they come to take him back to the Home, or to some new set of foster parents? He didn't trust himself to speak, so he just nodded.

The man put the briefcase carefully on the table. 'I've waited a long time to deliver this.' He undid the clasps and opened the lid. 'It's been kept safe in our vaults at New Scotland Yard for a very long time.'

Inside, the case was padded with dark foam to keep the contents safe and secure. The man lifted out a rectangle of foam to reveal a recess below. Resting in it was a plain white envelope, yellowed with age and addressed in faded black ink. It said simply, 'Ben Foundling – c/o Gibbet Manor'. The man had taken white cotton gloves from his jacket pocket. He slipped them on, then very carefully lifted the letter out of the case. Ben could see that on the back it was sealed with a blob of red wax.

'I have strict instructions to deliver this only to Ben Foundling at this address on this exact date.'

He handed Ben the letter.

'What do I do with it?'

The man took off his gloves and closed the briefcase. 'That's up to you. I've done my job.'

'But who's it from?' Rupam asked.

'I don't know. All I can tell you,' the man said, 'is that it's a Priority One Instruction I deliver the letter and that it's been in the secure police vaults since 1943.'

7

THE SUN WAS LOW IN THE SKY AND THE SPOTS of rain had turned to a persistent drizzle. Maria and Knight stood in the doorway of the pub, sheltering from the weather and considering their options. The church tower was again a ruined stump jutting above the treeline.

'We're sort of flickering in and out of reality. Or rather, the village is. We should tell the others what's happening,' Knight decided.

'Don't frighten Gemma,' Maria warned him. 'She only needs to know we're stuck here for a bit.'

'That's all we really know,' Knight pointed out.

They had tried the other road out of the village but never even got as far as the army checkpoint. A mass of greenery blocked the road, the hedges seeming to grow across the lane. Maria was scratched all over from trying to push through. But the vegetation formed an impenetrable barrier.

It was the same whichever way they tried – sooner or later, and usually sooner, they reached a wall of shrubs and trees, creepers and leaves . . .

'It's like we're trapped inside Sleeping Beauty's castle a hundred years on,' Maria said. 'We should have brought my sword.'

'It isn't actually yours,' Knight reminded her. 'Though I admit you're more accomplished with it than any of the rest of us. But you're right. There are a lot of things we should have brought. Hindsight is a wonderful thing.'

'Can we burn our way through?'

'Everything's too damp.' Knight checked his phone again. 'And even if we could send for a helicopter, I wouldn't risk an airlift. Assuming there's still room to land a helicopter, who knows what's really up there, circling above us, watching? There could be any kind of demon or creature. We need to get a message out.' He put his phone away and sighed. 'Come on, back to the church.'

'We'll get wet.'

'That's the least of our problems.' Knight stepped out into the rain. 'It's not that bad. Let's go.'

With a grunt of irritation, Maria followed him.

'If you're that bothered,' Knight told her, 'you can shelter in the phone box.'

He stopped abruptly and Maria almost walked into him.

'What is it?' She followed his gaze to the small phone box on the other side of the road. 'Like I said, it won't still be connected.'

Knight set off towards the phone box. 'It might be – if it thinks it's in 1943, like those soldiers. Like the pub when Tommy was here. Like the church tower . . .'

'You are kidding!' Maria tried to squeeze into the small cubicle behind Knight, but she was still getting wet from the rain. 'Anything?'

In answer, he held the chunky Bakelite phone receiver to her ear.

'Hello? Hello?' a woman's voice said impatiently. 'Is there anyone there? What number do you require? I haven't got all day. There's a war on, you know, so unless this is urgent please hang up.'

Knight replaced the handset.

'Interesting, but I'm not sure it helps. Who do we know in 1943 and what's their phone number?'

'We could call the police.'

'Even if they believe us, they'll come here nearly seventy years ago. That's no use. There must be a way,' he said thoughtfully. 'I must know a phone number that will help. Ah!' He clicked his fingers.

'What's the most famous phone number of the twentieth century?'

'Er . . . 999?' Maria said. 'Or 1066?'

'Very funny.' Knight lifted the receiver again. 'Hello? Can you get me a London number please? A reverse-charge call, is that the term?' He listened for a moment. 'Yes, I can wait. We're not going anywhere. And the number is Whitehall 1212.'

The letter was old and dry. It cracked as Ben pulled it out of the envelope and unfolded it.

'What's it say? Who's it from?' Rupam demanded.

'You should wait for Mrs Bailey to come back,' Sam said quietly.

She was sitting on the large circular wooden table in the middle of the library. Right where Rupam would have seen her – if she had really been there.

Mrs Bailey had taken the man with the briefcase back to his car. He was obviously disappointed not to discover what was in the letter he'd brought all the way from London.

'It's dated 3 March 1943,' Ben said as soon as Mrs Bailey returned. 'And it's a message from Mr Knight.'

3 March 1943

Dear Ben Foundling

I do not pretend to understand what is happening or why I have been asked to ensure that this letter is delivered to you so far in the future at such a remote location. But I have just spoken on the telephone with Mr Dirk Knight, who assures me that it is of the utmost importance that I follow his instructions. He was most persuasive and I am sure he has his reasons. The code words he used have been confirmed at the highest level.

I noted down exactly what Mr Knight asked me to tell you and will copy it exactly from my notes:

We are trapped in the village with no communications except this telephone. Greene's people at the checkpoints are under the same illusion as Corporal Rutherford and, I imagine, now believe they have orders to shoot on sight. Other ways out seem to be blocked by hedges and vegetation.

The solution must lie within the village itself.
The only clue we have is the words of an old
woman we met: 'Beware the green.' We have
no idea what she meant. Growl desperately
needs the documents Mrs Bailey has provided
to complete his research, plus whatever else you
have discovered.

While Mrs Bailey works with Captain Morton to
sort out Greene's people and organise satterlight
(sorry, not sure of the spelling – SB) surveillance
for Webbie, you and Rupam must bring the
documents and information to us here at the
village church.

Be careful. Don't try to come through the
checkpoints.

Oh, and Maria says it will be like trying to get
into Sleeping Beauty's castle, so bring a sword.
You know which one. Quick as you can.

Good luck.
Knight.

Although I suspect that by the time you receive
this letter I shall not be in a position to offer much

assistance, I remain, sir, your obedient servant,

Stephen Bircher

(Detective Chief Inspector)

The cellar was cold. Ben could feel the chill as soon as he started down the stone steps that led to the vault. He'd never been allowed through the huge circular metal door that sealed the vault off from the rest of the cellar. As it was, he didn't relish coming here. He wished Sam was with him, but she had disappeared somewhere on the way from the library.

Outside the vault was a large area filled with computer equipment. This was where Webby worked. Where he lived too, though he insisted it was only for a few more months until his contract ended. No one believed him – Webby had been here for years. It was his job to set up and maintain all the computer and network systems. Agents of the School of Night could get online training, report sightings of ghosts and other paranormal phenomena, send in data gathered on their mobile phones . . . Webby's systems monitored, collated and catalogued it all from his base down here in the cellar.

It was packed with computer equipment –

monitors, system units, disk drives, keyboards and mouses. It also smelt.

'Doesn't he ever wash?' Ben asked Rupam quietly as they descended the stairs.

'Who knows? I've never seen him wash. But I've never seen him sleep either.'

'Or eat?' Ben mused, seeing a plate of sandwiches on a table at the bottom of the stairs. The bread had dried and was beginning to curl.

'Busy man,' Rupam said.

Webby was plugged into his music player, tapping out a beat on a computer keyboard. He saw Rupam and Ben and gave them a 'just a minute' wave.

'Satellite's in position, at last,' Webby announced loudly, without removing his earphones. 'Got Captain Morton to thank for that. Had to retask a satellite that was watching the French navy – don't ask why. But anyway, we've been getting real-time images snapped every two minutes for a couple of hours now.' He pointed to a screen on the other side of the cellar. 'If you want proper video that costs more, apparently.'

The screen showed an aerial picture of Templeton. It looked as if it had been taken from a helicopter or a low-flying plane rather than a satellite high in orbit above the planet. Ben could see the church with its broken roof and separate, ruined tower. The road into the village forked close to what must be the pub.

'Can you see any people?' Rupam asked.

'Could if anyone was there,' Webby said, pulling out his earphones at last. 'Couple of people about earlier. Went off the side, up the lane, then came back again. They've gone now. No sign of Knight's car.'

'You can see how overgrown the place is,' Ben said, pointing to where a hedge seemed to be growing across the lane.

The village seemed to be hemmed in all round by a mass of green.

'Sleeping Beauty's castle,' Rupam said.

Webby spun round on his chair. 'Never mind that. There's nothing much to see. I've pulled some data and documents off the web, if you want to take a look at what I've found.'

Nothing seemed that interesting to Ben. Webby had managed to find various bits and pieces. There were several old Ordnance Survey maps of the area, census data from 1841 through to 1901, and the records from the Domesday Book compiled in 1086.

'Like that will help,' Ben muttered.

There was also a scanned copy of a pamphlet about

the history of the church written by the local rector in 1937, which Rupam said might interest Growl.

'I'd stick it all on a laptop, but I guess there's no power there.'

'Shouldn't think so,' Ben agreed.

'And you don't want to be carrying a stack of batteries round the place.'

'No, they won't.' Mrs Bailey's voice echoed down the stairs. Moments later she appeared, holding a tray with drinks on it. 'They'll have quite enough to carry as it is. I've put everything into a couple of rucksacks, though what you'll do with the sword is another matter.'

'Sword?' Webby asked.

'Doesn't matter,' Ben said, helping himself to a glass of milk from the tray. 'Thanks.'

Rupam had milk too. Mrs Bailey had brought mugs of steaming coffee for herself and Webby.

'Madam Sosostram will take you to Templeton,' Mrs Bailey told Ben and Rupam. 'I need to get in touch with Captain Morton again. There's an air exclusion zone over the village anyway, but he's extending that to include the military. The last thing we want is army helicopters and planes crashing into Grotesques or wind demons. And someone has to keep this place in order.'

'There's no sign of any aerial demons on the satellite images,' Rupam said, turning to look.

'There wouldn't be. It doesn't have a filter like your phone. I've got some readings here that are a bit dodgy, though,' Webby said, beating out a staccato rhythm on his keyboard.

'Careful!' Mrs Bailey called.

'What?' Rupam turned back.

Ben couldn't see what Mrs Bailey was warning them about either. But as Rupam turned again towards the screen showing the images from the satellite, his hand caught Webby's coffee cup, knocking it over.

The steaming liquid splashed over Webby's jeans. Ben expected him to leap up in pain, swearing and angry. But he seemed not to notice, still typing away.

'I'll get a cloth,' Mrs Bailey said.

'Sorry. But it's moved,' Rupam said.

They could all hear the urgency in his voice. Even Webby turned to look.

'What's moved?' Ben asked.

Rupam pointed to a hedge that crossed the road at one side of the screen. 'Here – it's moved slightly, I'm sure. And it's bigger than it was.'

'I haven't changed the zoom,' Webby said.

As he stood up, he seemed to notice the spilt coffee for the first time, brushing it off his jeans with irritation. Ben stepped back as Webby pushed past him. It wasn't just the cellar that smelt – Ben had caught a whiff of Webby himself. He *stank*. Not the usual pungent smell of sweat, but a sweet, almost sickly odour.

'I'm sure it's different,' Rupam was saying as Webby examined the picture.

'Can you rewind or something?' Ben wondered. 'Then we can see if there's a difference.'

'Better than that, I can play back a sequence of all the images since it came online.' Webby returned to his computer.

'Like time-lapse photography?' Mrs Bailey asked. 'Speeding up flowers opening, that sort of thing?'

The images started to play through, like a jerky video.

'Not just flowers,' Ben said.

Rupam was right. The hedge had moved and grown thicker. But it was not just that hedge. As they watched, the vegetation round the edge of the village thickened and moved, pressing inwards. Slowly but surely, the greenery was advancing on the centre of the village, blocking the roads and fields, cutting it off from the outside world. A mass of trees, shrubs, hedges, ivy – all types of vegetation – moving inexorably inwards.

'I think we should get going,' Ben said.

'What was it in Knight's letter – the warning from the old woman they met?' Sam said quietly. She was standing right beside him and Ben hadn't noticed.

Rupam hadn't heard Sam, but he was making the same connection. 'That's what it means,' he said. '*Beware the green.*'

8

BEN WONDERED IF MADAM SOSOSTRAM COULD drive. Mrs Bailey had said simply that the old woman would take them to Templeton village, but had given no indication of how she was going to do it. He couldn't imagine the frail old lady with her walking stick driving a car. If she did, it was likely to be as battered and ancient a wreck as the one Reverend Growl drove. In which case it would be a long, tedious and uncomfortable journey.

'Can she *drive*?' Rupam echoed incredulously when Ben asked. He burst out laughing. 'I think you have a lot to learn about Madam Sosostram. You see her as an elderly lady, that's all. But there is a lot more to her than that. There are other ways to see her.'

'What do you mean?'

'Just that you are in for a surprise.' Rupam wouldn't say any more than that.

Ben's first surprise came as they waited outside

the front door of Gibbet Manor, each with a rucksack stuffed with books and papers from Mrs Bailey, plus printouts from Webby. Rupam was holding a long, thin silver sword with an ornate handle and wrist-guard. Ben didn't know how – or if – the metal had been treated, but he knew from watching Maria use it that the sword could cut through invisible demons and Grotesques . . .

A bright red sports car roared round the side of the house and crunched to a halt. It had an open top and a bonnet that dipped so low it almost touched the ground. The engine throbbed and growled, but it was barely audible as rock music was blasting out from the car's hi-fi system. Two huge black speakers were mounted in the back of the car. They vibrated with the noise pumping through them.

'Put your bags in the front, boys,' Madam Sosostram said, turning down the music. 'You can both sit in the back. I'm sure neither of you wants to have to make conversation with an old fossil like me.'

It was odd to see the old lady driving a sports car. She had her woolly cardigan tightly buttoned and her grey hair had been blown back. She watched Ben and Rupam through horn-rimmed spectacles as they dumped their rucksacks on the front seat. Rupam leaned the silver sword against the seat, angled away from the gear stick. Then they had to climb over the back of the car to get in, moving Madam Sosostram's walking stick out of the way before they could sit down.

With a wizened smile of approval, Madam Sosotram turned up the volume again, put the car into gear and sprayed gravel across the driveway as she floored the accelerator.

The car roared down the drive, Bon Jovi blasting out.

It was difficult to speak in the car with all the noise from the music and the powerful engine. Rupam seemed to spend most of the journey grinning at Ben.

'What?' Ben yelled at last.

Rupam's grin broadened.

'What?'

Ben found himself grinning too. He knew what Rupam found so funny. It wasn't just his surprise, it was the fact that they were being driven through the countryside in a red convertible sports car by a little old lady who played rock music far too loud and had no worries about breaking the speed limit.

They shot through a town, the buildings

blurring past. Two young men in hoodies watched them. One gave a thumbs-up and the other waved. Madam Sosostram gave a cheery wave back.

'If only they knew,' Rupam shouted in Ben's ear.

'Yeah, right.' But Ben wasn't sure what Rupam meant. 'They probably think she's our granny,' he yelled.

Rupam was grinning again and shaking his head. It wasn't until they reached the army checkpoint that Ben found out why.

An olive-green army Land Rover was parked across the road. Two soldiers stood beside it. One of them stepped forward, hand up to signal the car to stop.

Madam Sosostram cut the music. 'Duck down, boys. Don't let them see you.'

'What are we going to do – crash through the roadblock?' Ben could believe that anything was possible.

'I'll distract the soldiers. As soon as you get a chance, see if you can get past.'

'What about you?' Rupam hissed.

Madam Sosostram opened the door and heaved her ample form awkwardly out of the car. 'I think I shall probably be stuck here on this side of the cordon.'

Ben peered out carefully through the gap between the driver's seat and its headrest. The soldier was approaching and Madam Sosostram hobbled towards him.

'How's she going to distract them?' Ben whispered to Rupam.

'Don't look too closely. Try not to focus.'

'What do you mean?'

'You know those pictures that look like a mess of jumbled colours?' Rupam asked quietly. 'And if you focus beyond them, let your eyes sort of relax, then a three-dimensional shape appears?'

'I can never do that,' Ben admitted.

'Well, try again. Try now. And you'll see what the soldiers can see – what Madam Sosostram *wants* them to see.'

Ben tried it. Madam Sosostram had met the soldier halfway between the car and the Land Rover. The other soldier was walking over slowly to join them, grinning. Madam Sosostram laughed at something the first soldier said. She tilted her head back, pushing a curl of white hair behind her ear. It was a strange movement for the old woman.

'Can you see it yet?'

Ben shook his head. 'I don't know what you mean.'

Madam Sosostram was walking towards the

Land Rover, the soldiers walking with her. She placed one hand on the bonnet of the vehicle, leaning over it. There was something odd about the way she had walked, Ben thought – her limp was gone. There was a confidence to her movements that he hadn't noticed before. And the way she leaned towards the soldier, hand still on the bonnet . . .

As if she was a young woman, not an old lady.

A young woman.

Ben gasped. He rose up out of the seat to get a better view, but Rupam pulled him down out of sight.

'You see it now, don't you?' He was grinning again.

Ben *did* see it. As he let his eyes relax, the ungainly figure of Madam Sosostram faded, shimmered and changed. She grew slimmer, her tweedy skirt and jacket somehow becoming an elegant, low-cut dress. Her flat shoes were knee-length boots with chunky heels. Her white curls extended into long, straight, gold-blonde hair. She glanced back over her shoulder and Ben saw that she had eyes like a cat's, the deepest green. Her skin was no longer old and wrinkled. She was a stunningly beautiful young woman in her mid-twenties.

'She lets us see her how she really is. But that – that's how everyone else sees her. The soldiers, those hoodies in the town, everyone. Well, if she wants them to.'

Ben just stared. 'I saw her,' he remembered. 'Soon after I came to the School of Night – I saw her like that and I never even realised it was her.'

'Maybe she didn't know you were watching. I guess it's a habit, keeping up the appearance. Hey – come on,' Rupam said, climbing quickly and quietly out of the back of the car.

The young woman who was Madam Sosostram had walked slowly round behind the Land Rover and the two soldiers were following her. Ben heard laughter again – the laughter of the soldiers and of a young woman.

He grabbed his rucksack from the front of the car and ran after Rupam to take cover behind the Land Rover, hidden on the opposite side to the soldiers.

Madam Sosostram appeared at the back of the vehicle. She glanced quickly at Ben and Rupam, then gave a curt nod. The boys edged round as Madam Sosostram led the two soldiers back towards her car.

'Restricted area?' Ben heard her saying – her

voice was strong and light at the same time, almost musical. 'That sounds *very* exciting. I am sorry to have distracted you, but thank you *so* much for the directions to Dorchester. If I get lost, I'll just have to come back here and try again, won't I?'

On the other side of the roadblock, Ben gripped his rucksack tight and ran. He sank down beside Rupam at the edge of the road. The soldiers were watching as an old lady in a red sports car executed a rapid three-point turn in the narrow lane, then roared off into the distance, the music of the Prodigy echoing in her wake.

With the soldiers back the other side of the roadblock, Ben and Rupam were able to get out of sight beyond the bend in the road.

'How far is it to Templeton, do you think?' Ben wondered.

The sword was now strapped to the back of Rupam's rucksack, sticking out either side. It almost hit Ben as Rupam turned. 'No idea.'

'Hey! Careful with that.'

'Sorry. I think that was a sort of outer checkpoint. We're further out than the satellite image showed.'

'And those soldiers didn't seem to think they were fighting the Second World War,' Ben added.

They slowed to a walking pace as soon as they were out of sight of the roadblock.

'How do you do it?' Ben asked after a while.

'Do what?'

'Remember things.'

'Oh, that.'

They went on in silence. They seemed to be walking forever. It was difficult to get any idea of where they were because high hedges now rose on either side of the narrow road. Ben wondered if Rupam was going to answer his question or not. Maybe he'd offended his friend in some way.

'I just wondered,' Ben said after a while. 'Sorry.'

'No, that's OK. I was trying to think of how to answer. You can train yourself to have a good memory. But I just sort of do it. There's . . .' He paused, frowning. 'There's a place I go,' Rupam said at last.

'A place? To remember?'

'Not a real place. It's inside my mind. In my imagination. It's always been there. Maybe it was somewhere I used to know. I . . .' He laughed suddenly. 'I can't remember.'

'You remember everything,' Ben joked. Except, of course, it was true.

'Yes. But I mean I can't remember a time when I

didn't remember everything, when the place wasn't in my head.'

'This place – how does it work?'

'It's like a big house. Bigger than that – enormous. A palace. There are so many rooms, and there's a garden too, with lots of areas. And there are things in the palace. All the things I want to remember. It's not like a movie I can replay – some people remember that way. There's no set sequence to it. I put things in the rooms of the palace.'

'What, like lists of things? Stuff we have to learn? Whole books?'

'Yes. Or things that jog my memory rather than the actual things to remember. I say I put them there, and some of them I do, but others just *are*. If I read something, then afterwards it's there – whether I choose to put it in or not.'

Ben nodded. It sort of made sense. People kept notes, or tied knots in their handkerchiefs to remind them of things. That was sort of what Rupam did, only in his mind and on a grander – and more successful – scale.

'But don't you have to remember which room it's in?' Ben asked.

'I just know. I go to the right room in my head and what I need is in there. So, if I need to remember the look on your face when you saw Madam Sosostram change, I go to the third room on the left down the corridor from the stairs on the third floor.'

'And the look on my face is in there?'

'There's a photo album,' Rupam said. He was staring into space as they walked. 'It's on a small table beside a bookcase. I turn the page and there's your expression. Like a photograph. Looking back at me.' He laughed. 'You should see it!'

'Maybe I will,' Ben told him. 'Maybe one day I'll come to your memory palace and you can show me round.'

'No,' Rupam said sharply. 'No – never go there. There are some rooms that you don't want to see. Some rooms even I don't want to go into.' He quickened his pace. 'Some rooms I wish did not exist. Rooms you might never leave.'

From his tone, Ben could tell the conversation was over. He wasn't sure if he should have asked or not. He looked round, half expecting to see Sam, half expecting her to tell him it was OK. But she wasn't there. Ben hurried to catch up as his friend rounded another corner.

Rupam had stopped. He was standing in front of a high, dense hedge that was growing across the road. Ben stood beside him as they stared at it. He could see brambles and bindweed threading through the branches. The sun was low in the sky behind the hedge, but there was no sign of light shining through.

'Well, we know there's no way round it,' Ben said. 'I wonder if it's growing as quickly as it seems to be on the satellite pictures.'

'I don't want to stay here long enough to find out,' Rupam said. 'I guess this is why we brought the sword. Help me get it out, will you?'

Ben unstrapped the sword and handed it to Rupam.

'Are you going to hack a way through?'

Rupam raised the sword. 'Unless you think we can just push our way to the other side? It could be several metres thick by now. Stand back.'

'I hope you know what you're doing,' Ben muttered, keeping well out of the way.

Rupam swung the sword down and it sliced through the branches and leaves easily. Soon he had cut deep into the hedge. He stepped in among the greenery, still hacking away. His blows were not so effective now as he had less room to swing the blade. But he was working his way deeper and deeper into the mass of vegetation.

Ben followed at a safe distance. It was almost dark inside the tunnel that was being created and soon he could hardly see Rupam. The blade glinted as it caught what little light there was. He could hear it thwacking into the branches as Rupam forced his way through.

Ben glanced back, wondering how far they had come. Behind him, the opening had dwindled to almost nothing. Surely it wasn't that far? As he watched, the gap closed up completely.

'Rupam!' Ben called, suddenly afraid. 'We need to hurry.'

'I'm going as quickly as I can.'

'But – it's growing back!' Ben shouted. 'The hedge is growing back and we'll be trapped inside if we don't get through soon.'

The sword slashed with renewed vigour. Ben hurried to catch up with Rupam, but his foot caught in the loop of a branch and he went sprawling to the ground. Brambles scratched at his face and hands as he struggled up again. Leaves battered his eyes and he tried to brush them away, but they seemed to catch in his fingers, curling, entwining. A branch lashed out and smacked into his legs. A long creeper shot up from among the greenery, wrapping itself round his thigh and squeezing painfully tight.

'Ben!' Rupam's voice was muffled. 'Ben, it's moving. It's *alive!*'

A mass of grass and nettles seemed to rear up in front of Ben, hurtling towards him like a wild animal – clawing, scratching, stinging and tearing at his skin as he tried to fight it off. Pressing into his mouth. His eyes. He was dragged down into the soft leaves. The last of the light disappeared and everything went dark green.

9

SILVER IN THE DARKNESS. A FLASH OF LIGHT CUT across Ben's vision. There was a tightness about his throat – strands gripping and squeezing. Was that why he was seeing a flashing light?

But the tightness was loosening. He managed to work his fingers under the bindweed that was strangling him, ripping it away. Someone else was pulling brambles and roots and branches away from him. A hand reached out of the darkness – barely visible – dragging him to his feet.

'Rupam?' Ben managed to gasp.

'Who were you expecting?' Rupam was out of breath. His sword flashed again in the near-darkness, carving out a path before him. 'Thought I'd lost you.'

'I thought I'd lost *you*.'

Ben tried to keep close as his friend hacked a way through. Leaves still whipped at his face, while roots continued to thrust out from the ground and stab at his feet. Branches twisted round his legs and arms. But Ben managed to fight them all off and stumble after Rupam.

Several times they fell. Several times Ben had to drag vegetation off Rupam as it threatened to overwhelm him and drown him in a mass of green. Several times Rupam did the same for him.

It seemed an eternity before they saw the faintest glimmer of sunlight shining through the blanket of greenery. With renewed enthusiasm and hope they forced their way towards the light.

And suddenly they were out of the hedge. They pitched forward on to the roadway on the other side, gasping for breath, laughing with relief. Then they staggered to their feet and stumbled down the road, desperate to get as far away as possible. Tendrils of ivy twitched in the hedges at either side of the road, as if watching the two boys as they ran past.

Maria was sitting on the remains of a stone wall close to the phone box opposite the pub.

'You took your time,' she told Ben and Rupam as they ran up, breathless. 'Still,' she went on, pushing herself off the wall, 'at least it's stopped raining. You got our message, then?'

'Obviously,' Ben said.

Maria ignored him. She'd seen that Rupam was

holding the sword and took it from him. 'What have you been doing? It's filthy.'

She wiped the blade on the damp grass verge.

'We had a bit of trouble,' Rupam said.

'With a hedge,' Ben added.

Maria nodded. 'You look like you got dragged through it backwards.' She turned and marched off towards the church. 'Come on. Everyone's been waiting.'

'Do you know the story of why the tower's separate from the church?' Rupam asked as they walked through the overgrown graveyard.

The sun was low in the sky now, shining across the wet grass and ragged-looking gravestones.

'It's because the tower is older. Some sort of fortification,' Maria said. 'Growl researched it before we came here.'

'I said did you know the *story*, not the truth,' Rupam said, but Maria was already striding ahead impatiently.

The vestry was too small for all six of them to crowd into. Growl was working at a desk already covered with open books and handwritten notes, while Gemma and Knight were helping.

'I suggest we adjourn,' Growl said, 'to somewhere better suited to our investigations.'

'The pub?' Knight suggested.

'I was thinking of the school actually.' His eyes twinkled in the fading light and for a moment he was less serious and irascible. 'A good place to learn the truth, don't you think?'

As Growl and Knight gathered up the notes and papers, Rupam and Ben told them how they had received Knight's message, and all about the trouble they'd had getting into the village. Ben was not surprised that Knight in particular seemed to take the notion of being attacked by plants and shrubs and hedges in his stride.

'Things are becoming more urgent,' he said. 'I wonder how long we have before the vegetation closes right in and smothers the village entirely.'

'Pleasant thought,' Maria muttered. She gripped her sword purposefully. 'Do we fight our way out?'

'No, no, no,' Growl snapped. 'Absolutely not. The answers we need are here in this village. Abandon it and we lose control – we sacrifice the chance to learn the truth and put a stop to this.'

Rupam and Ben were the last to leave, following the others out through the ruined church. Gemma waited for them at the main door.

'I'm glad you're here,' she told the boys.

'At least someone is,' Ben said. He was feeling

ignored and unappreciated, and guessed Rupam felt the same. 'We come all this way, we get half killed and no one's even said thank you.'

'You'd better get used to it,' Rupam said, forcing a smile.

Gemma gave Ben a quick hug, then embraced Rupam. 'We're all glad you're here. It's just that some of us don't show it. Growl is . . . well, Growl, and Mr Knight never tells anyone they've done well.'

'And Maria?' Ben said.

Gemma raised her eyebrows, as if to ask whether that was a serious question.

The sun had dipped below the horizon by the time they arrived at the school. It was a single-storey Victorian building with a steep roof – most of which was still in place. Tiles had slipped off, though, and there were patches where the rafters were exposed.

Inside was a small foyer which led into an office area on one side and the main schoolroom on the other. The schoolroom took up most of the building. It was large and rectangular, reaching up the full height of the building. The ceiling was discoloured and plaster had broken away, falling over the desks and floor.

The end of the room was raised up a step to create an area for the teacher. On this low dais stood a desk, a blackboard – with the date 24 February 1943 still faintly visible – and an upright chair. The walls had been whitewashed, but were spattered with patches of damp. There were several faded posters, one with pictures and names of farm animals. Another showed each of the letters of the alphabet beside something starting with that letter. It was headed 'Phonics'.

'I thought that was a new thing,' Maria said.

'Nothing new under the sun,' Growl told her. 'Old wine in new bottles.'

Each desk had a bench seat attached to it. Knight got everyone to help turn the desks and position them to form a long single table with a bench running down each side. Growl spread his papers out again, then Rupam and Ben piled the material from their rucksacks at the end of this makeshift table.

'I hope they won't mind us moving their desks,' Gemma said.

Ben couldn't see what she meant, until he opened his mobile phone. Then he saw the faint impressions of the children, sitting now along both sides of the table. Girls in pinafore dresses and boys in shorts and grubby shirts turned to look at him.

The teacher – a middle-aged lady with her hair in a severe bun – rapped on the blackboard with a cane for the children's attention.

Ben closed his phone. 'Do you see them all the time?' he asked Gemma quietly.

She nodded, biting her lower lip. 'Rupam knows they're there, but he doesn't actually see them. Maria does, though.'

Ben glanced across at the older girl. She was staring at the table, or rather at the children Ben could no longer see sitting round it. Her face was pale and she blinked back tears from her eyes. Then she caught sight of Ben. He looked away.

'What are you staring at?' Maria demanded. 'There must be some lamps somewhere,' she said, pushing past him and hurrying from the room.

'Yes, that would be useful,' Growl said, still arranging his documents.

There were no lamps, but Maria found a drawer full of candles in the office. With Gemma's help, she carried them through. They also found school registers dating back to 1907, which Growl accepted with enthusiasm and added to his collection of books, documents and printouts.

Rupam and Ben helped position the candles round the schoolroom and down the middle of the table.

Knight had a lighter, though Ben had never seen him smoke. Once a candle was lit, Ben let it burn for a few seconds to melt enough wax for him to tip out and use to glue the candle in place once it set.

It was only when Knight suggested that Ben and the other children get some sleep while he and Growl continued their work that Ben realised how tired he was. It was late and dark. Gemma was yawning and Rupam had slumped against the wall at the side of the raised dais.

'I'm not tired,' Maria said.

'Nevertheless,' Knight told her, 'I'd like you to sort out the others. I suggest you bed down in the office as best you can. I think I saw some blankets in there.'

'They're tablecloths,' Maria told him. But she didn't argue.

There was just about room for them to lie down, each wrapped up in a couple of tablecloths, on the office floor. It was uncomfortable, but Ben was too tired to wriggle about and try to improve things. He'd slept in worse places, he thought. A single candle gave them faint, flickering light as they all settled down.

'Tell us the story of the church tower,' Maria said.

'What story?' Gemma wanted to know. She

sounded half asleep.

'It's interesting,' Rupam said. 'As you know, the real reason the church tower is separate from the main building is because it's older. It was probably part of another church, or maybe a fortification of some sort that no longer exists.'

'So why build the new church away from the existing tower?' Ben asked.

'I don't know. Maybe there were ruins still in the way. It was originally a pagan site, centuries before. A lot of churches were built on land that was already thought to be sacred from earlier religions. But maybe they didn't want to associate too closely with that earlier religion here when they rebuilt the church.'

'Growl said much the same.' Maria sounded impatient. 'You said there was a story. We know the history, or as much as we want to anyway.'

'OK, OK. The story, or legend, doesn't care for the real history. In the story the church and tower were built at the same time and the tower joined the church. And the church was built near a site where the Devil was worshipped. He wanted his own church, but the villagers wouldn't build it for him. So he took the church tower and moved it to where he wanted it.'

'So is that why it's separate?' Ben asked.

'Just about. In the story, the villagers dismantled the tower and moved it back, rebuilding it attached to the church. But the next day the Devil had moved it again. So again the villagers pulled it down and rebuilt it with the church, and this time they carved statues of saints all round the tower to protect it.'

'I've seen the alcoves where the statues used to be,' Maria said.

'And the Devil still moved the tower?' Ben said.

'I guess so,' Rupam agreed. 'It's not attached to the church, so I suppose the villagers gave up. It's just a story,' he added.

But Ben hardly heard him. He was drifting into a dreamless sleep. The last things he was aware of were Maria saying something, Rupam laughing, the sound of Gemma's regular breathing from somewhere nearby . . . And his sister Sam's gentle kiss on his forehead as she said goodnight.

'Beware the green.' Reverend Growl stood by the blackboard, looking down at everyone else like the class teacher.

Ben sat with Rupam and Maria at the desks arranged into a long table. Gemma was perched on the other side, sitting on the desk, her feet on the bench seat and her chin resting on her knees. She looked bored. Knight stood leaning against the wall, arms folded.

'After the experiences of young Ben and Rupam yesterday, and our own observations of the approaching vegetation and plants, I think we now know what that warning means,' Growl said.

'Is that why the villagers are appearing?' Knight asked. 'Are they manifesting as some sort of warning?'

'Quite possibly,' Growl agreed. 'Let me tell you what my nocturnal studies have unearthed, then I think things will become a little clearer.'

'About time,' Maria muttered.

The early morning sunlight was angling in through the dusty windows of the schoolroom. A shadow fell across the table in front of Ben and he turned to see Sam standing behind him. She smiled, putting her finger to her lips.

'From the way the plants are growing and advancing, and from the satellite printouts that Webby provided showing a ring of vegetation round the village, it's very clear that the church is right in the middle. Here in the school we are close to the edge of the village, but the church is the epicentre if you like.'

'Does that mean the church itself is the key to

the problem?' Knight asked.

'Possibly. Or it may just be coincidence. The church is in the middle of the village after all. And even if this was entirely random, something would have to be in the middle of it.'

Growl picked up the printout of the pamphlet about the history of the church that Rupam had brought. 'This is the best source of information we've got. It was written in 1937, so it's as up to date as we're likely to find. There are a few line drawings, like this one of the tower.'

He held it up, but it was too far away for the others to see any detail.

Oblivious to this, Growl went on, 'Now, it's interesting, as this would appear to show the tower as it was before the Puritans vandalised it. But more of that in a moment.'

He turned to another page of the printout. 'We do learn a few interesting things, though I doubt they are relevant. But did you know that one of the graves in the churchyard is arranged north–south, rather than the traditional east–west that the other graves follow?'

'So what?' Sam said, though no one but Ben could hear her.

'Why is that important?' Ben asked.

'It quite possibly isn't important at all,' Growl admitted. 'But let us now turn our attention to the name of this village.'

'Templeton,' Rupam said.

'And why do you suppose it is called that?' There was no reply, so Growl continued, 'I'll tell you. It's because the Knights Templar had a temple here. Oh, a long time ago, and all trace of it has long since gone. No one is even sure quite where it was, though there are several mentions in the history of a "Temple of the Holy Crystal". But, more to the point, where you find the Knights Templar, it is not unusual to find the Memento Mori.'

Ben had heard of the Knights Templar long ago. More recently he had heard of the Memento Mori too. They were a secret order of priestly knights that answered directly to the Vatican – to the Pope. They fought against the powers of darkness – rather like the School of Night did now. The order had been dissolved in the early eighteenth century, but while they existed they were a powerful secret force for the Church.

'Memento Mori knights were buried facing north,' Knight said. 'Are you telling us that one of them is buried in the churchyard?'

'It's an interesting connection, isn't it?'

'They were buried facing north so that they would not go straight to Heaven,' Rupam said, quoting – Ben guessed – from one of Growl's own lectures. 'That way they could guide others through limbo to paradise.'

'It was also a sign that the knight's work on earth was unfinished,' Growl said, nodding his appreciation of Rupam's comment. 'Not all the knights of the Memento Mori were buried in this way, but many of them were if they had fallen in battle.'

'There was a battle here?' Gemma said, seeming interested for the first time.

'Not a conventional battle. But a spiritual one perhaps. And, as I say, it may not be significant. Rather more pertinent, I suspect, is the fact that the church is built on a pagan site. That's not unusual, of course. In fact there is a story about why the tower is separate from the church that relates back to the legend.'

'Rupam told us,' Gemma said. 'The Devil moved the tower.'

'Quite so. Well, in the legend.'

'As you say,' Knight interrupted, 'it isn't unusual for churches to be built on sites associated with earlier gods and religions.'

'Ah, but this site, where the church is now, was

associated with the very fertility of the land, with the rites of spring. I believe we're dealing with the Green Man. It's a surprisingly modern term in literature – just seventy years old in fact – but the ideas go back into the depths of time. To all intents and purposes this is where ancient people worshipped him. The Green Man was a personification of nature itself . . . the god representing earth and vegetation and the seasons, if you like.'

'Beware the green,' Knight said.

'The pub's called the Green Man,' Ben realised. 'I thought it was, like, Robin Hood.'

The sunlight on the desk in front of him was making a dappled pattern, illuminating some of the papers spread out there, leaving others in shadow.

'But the pub's much older than that,' Maria pointed out.

'True. That's because the name was around for a long time before it was used in literature and written down. It was there in local myths and legends, in folk tales and oral tradition. In the ancient carvings round the church tower you can still see what are called "foliate heads". These days they are quite openly known as the Green Man.'

'On the church tower?' Rupam echoed in surprise. His face dipped into shadow as he leaned forward.

'Which brings us back to the Puritans. They really didn't like worshipping God in the beauty of holiness, as the Bible has it. They wanted to do away with all that pomp and ceremony and keep things plain and simple. They destroyed stained-glass windows, ornate carvings, paintings. Someone probably whitewashed over that doom painting in the church to hide it. The Puritans would have removed the statues of saints from the alcoves round the church tower and smashed them.'

'Why is that important?' Ben asked.

The whole table was in shadow now. The sun must have gone behind a cloud. There was a scraping sound, as if a bird had landed on the roof above.

'Probably because of the history of the site, the saints were depicted with their feet resting on foliate heads. Literally crushing the Green Man underfoot.'

'Now the saints are gone, destroyed by the Puritans,' Maria said.

Growl nodded. 'But the foliate heads are still there. The Green Man is no longer being controlled – no longer under the heel of the saints and kept in thrall to the new order of the world.'

There was silence for several moments while they absorbed this information. And as they sat thinking, darkness crept across the floor, the shadows deepening.

'But you said the statues of the saints, which somehow kept the power of the Green Man in check, were destroyed by the Puritans,' Ben said, puzzled. 'When was that?'

'Oh, in the 1650s, I would think.'

'So why is there a problem now?'

Everyone looked to Growl.

'I'm afraid I have no idea,' he said.

Sam leaned forward, over Ben's shoulder. 'It's getting dark,' she said. 'How can it be getting dark?'

Ben frowned. She was right. He thought the sun had gone in, but it shouldn't be this dark.

'It's getting dark,' he said out loud, looking up at the windows set high in the walls above.

The glass in them was dulled and veined, like leaves. Greenery was spread across the panes – ivy and creepers growing over them, branches pressing against them.

Gemma jumped down off the desk. Maria and Rupam stood up, staring at the windows in horror.

'Has that grown while we've been talking?' Maria said.

'I think we should get out of here,' Knight decided.

One of the windows cracked across the middle,

making a sound like gunshot. Glass showered down into the schoolroom. Gemma shrieked as fragments lodged in her hair.

'Definitely,' Growl agreed. 'Out now!'

As they ran for the door at the back of the room, a tangle of greenery crashed in through the broken window. Creepers slithered down the wall like snakes, while vines snaked across the floor. There was an explosion of glass as another window collapsed in fragments. Bits of window frame whipped at Ben's face as he ran.

Knight heaved open the door . . .

Only to reveal a mass of green. Damp, glistening, pulsating, it bulged into the room. Ben could see buds bursting into small flowers. Tendrils extended and thickened. Branches lashed about, hunting for Ben and his friends as they backed away.

Then the weight of the vegetation pressing down on the roof finally caused the beams to give way. A canopy of green burst through and fell like a thorny blanket, knocking Ben off his feet and sending Rupam flying. Glass crunched as they landed and brambles dug into their flesh. The whole school was alive with thrashing plants and they were trapped inside.

10

BEN KNEW THAT HE WAS BEING SMOTHERED. HE fought back as best he could, ripping tendrils away from his face and pushing branches to the side, but he could feel himself getting weaker and weaker. Suddenly a hand reached through the mass of writhing vegetation. Ben grabbed it and was hauled to his feet.

He found himself staring into Growl's face. The clergyman was pale with anger.

'Get out of here,' he hissed at Ben. 'Any way you can, but just get out.'

Growl was holding a small prayer book in his hand and he thrust it out in front of him as he turned away. Ben could see the man muttering under his breath as he walked slowly forward. The greenery seemed to part for him, drawing back as if in fear. But before Ben could follow, it closed immediately behind him and Growl disappeared into the living forest.

'Ben!' Rupam staggered up to him. The boy's face was scratched and his hands were bleeding. 'We have to get out of here. Somehow.'

Rupam stumbled as his foot was dragged from under him. Ben grabbed his friend and with all his strength tore him free.

'Where are the others?'

'I saw Maria and Gemma. Maria's got the sword. She's hacking her way out.'

'Bet she's better with it than you,' Ben tried to joke.

'Much better.'

'Growl went through there,' Ben said, pointing. There was no way they could follow.

'Knight can look after himself.'

'He'll have to.'

All the time they were talking, Ben was looking for a way out – the slightest break in the vegetation hemming them in, the faintest light from beyond the wall of green. They had to fight just to stay on their feet, pulling away the branches and creepers that tried to bind them, kicking free of the roots that wanted to ensnare them . . .

In desperation, Ben looked to the heavens. Movement caught his eye – not the green of the plants this time, but artificial grey and white. A shirt beneath a suit. Knight was climbing up a massive branch that had forced its way through the window and dipped down into the greenery below. As Ben watched, Knight thrust smaller branches out of the way and tore at the thrashing leaves. Looking down, he saw Ben and Rupam.

'The others are out,' Knight yelled. 'See if you can get up here. We can climb over the top. It's the only way left.'

'We're right behind you,' Rupam shouted back.

Knight didn't hear because at that moment a huge creeper whipped across and lashed into his shoulder. He lost his grip on the branch he was climbing. For a moment Ben was sure he was going to fall, but at the last minute Knight managed to regain his balance. He looked down at the two boys, smiled and nodded. The creeper had drawn back, like an attacking cobra. It gathered itself and lashed out again.

But its prey was no longer there. Knight leapt from the branch, straight at the window. The last of the glass shattered as he crashed through. A mass of ivy slithered rapidly after him.

Ben and Rupam went up together, helping each other. The huge branch that Knight had climbed bucked under them like a fairground ride as it tried to shake them off.

'How does it know we're here?' Rupam asked as he clung on desperately. 'Can it *see*?'

'It just knows. Maybe it can feel us. Plants react to their surroundings, don't they?' Ben reasoned. 'Maybe it can sense us from our temperature or the damp of our sweat or something. Anyway, does it matter?' he demanded, as he lost his grip and almost fell.

'Does if we can hide from the plants somehow,' Rupam said.

His words were muffled by the ivy threading its way over his face and trying to get into his mouth. He bit and spat, and finally managed to hold on with one hand while using the other to tear the ivy away.

Ben was faring no better. After every few inches he climbed, he had to stop and drag aside the greenery that was struggling to hold him back. He kicked out at the creepers that tightened round his feet and legs. Scratched away the ivy and leaves. Tried to avoid the thrashing brambles.

Below, he could see the ruins of the desks. The papers and printouts that he and Rupam had risked their lives to get to Knight were ripped to pieces. The desks themselves had been torn apart or crushed. A stem erupted through an old inkwell, stabbing towards Ben. He grabbed for a higher branch, kicked at a foothold and hauled himself upwards.

Above him, Rupam was now straddling the remains of the window ledge. Spikes of glass still clung to the sides of the window frame, glittering in the filtered sunlight. Rupam reached down for Ben. Their fingertips touched. Ben forced himself upright. His fingers curled round Rupam's.

Finally, they were both at the window. The ground seemed to be rushing up to meet them. The floor of the schoolroom was a green blanket, billowing higher and higher.

Hands linked, Ben and Rupam jumped into space.

And now the plants that were trying to kill them saved their lives.

Ben tumbled into a soft canopy of greenery. The branches and leaves of a yew tree broke and slowed his fall. He caught a confused glimpse of Rupam – all arms and legs – spinning past him. Ben grabbed at the branches, leaves and twigs – anything to slow his descent.

At last he rolled clear, on to a patch of ordinary grass. Breathing heavily, he lay on his back, staring up at the pale blue sky. He was worn out. He didn't move until he felt the grass under his hands stir and start to grow. As tendrils of green crept across his exhausted body, Ben dragged himself to his feet.

Rupam was standing a short distance away, staring back at the wall of matted vegetation that completely covered the school building.

'Where are the others?' Ben asked, hurrying to join him.

Rupam shook his head. 'The ground is moving. We need to get away from here.'

'No kidding.'

But which way should they go? Ben was disorientated from the escape and had no idea which window they had tumbled out of. All he could see was the sudden impossible plant life shooting up around them. He couldn't recognise any of the features of the school – even the main doors.

'This way,' Rupam decided.

'How do you know?' Ben ran after him.

'I don't. But the jungle is thinner here. It must be the way back to the middle of the village, to the church.'

Ben hadn't thought of it as a jungle. But now Rupam used the word, he realised that was what it was – a jungle of English trees and plants, shrubs and creepers.

They ran as fast as they could, crashing through

the hedges and walls of green. They tripped and fell, helped each other up and staggered on. They felt the cruel thorns of the brambles and climbing roses, the whiplash cuts of narrow willow leaves and the stab of branches.

They ran until the world solidified around them, slowing their progress. Then they forced their way through – heads down, shouldering aside the curtains of foliage. Pushing through the undergrowth was like wading through water. Ben and Rupam linked arms so they wouldn't get separated and forged ahead.

Not daring to stop, they carried on, slower and slower, until both of them were near to total exhaustion. Ben was about to collapse when he saw Rupam suddenly grin.

'We're through!' Rupam exclaimed. 'Look – we're through!' And now he was laughing as he dragged Ben onwards.

The jungle stopped. An abrupt wall of green rose up like a hedge behind them as Ben and Rupam staggered through it and flopped to the ground. To the grass. To the normal, damp grass that didn't move under them or curl upwards at them . . .

For a full minute, they lay panting on their backs, staring at the sky.

Until a green shape loomed massively above them. Ben leapt to his feet.

'Hey, steady on. Are you OK?'

The shape was a soldier in khaki uniform, his face smeared with dark camouflage paint. Plastic leaves stuck out from the webbing on his helmet. He cradled an assault rifle.

'What were you doing in there? How did you *get* here? This is a restricted area.'

'And you're going to tell us it's 1943 and don't we know there's a war on,' Ben gasped, still out of breath.

The soldier gave a short bark of laughter. 'Am I hell? Who do you think I am?' He shook his head and turned to glance at several other soldiers hurrying over to join them. 'God knows what Colonel Greene's going to say when he hears about this.'

'Where did these kids come from?' another soldier asked, jogging up. He had the three stripes of a sergeant on his shoulder.

'No idea, Sarge. They just appeared out of the hedge.'

'We have to get back in there, reach the village,' Ben said. 'We've got to help Mr Knight and the others.'

'What's he on about, Cooper?' the sergeant demanded.

The first soldier – Cooper – shook his head.

'Please,' Rupam begged. 'We only just got out, through there.' He pointed back at the wall of greenery. From this side it just looked like a hedge. 'It's growing,' he said. 'It attacked us.'

The two soldiers looked at each other.

'The hedge attacked you?' the sergeant said. 'Yeah, right. Get these two back to HQ,' he told Cooper. 'The colonel will want a word with them.'

'Yes, Sarge.'

'Rupam's right,' Ben insisted. 'You have to listen to us, please.'

His words were drowned out by the noise of a powerful engine. A large tank rumbled into view, its tracks chewing up the grass. Its heavy gun seemed to be aiming right at Ben and Rupam. Moments later, a second tank swept up alongside, then a third. They stopped about twenty metres from where the boys were standing.

'Please,' Ben said again as the tanks' engines idled more quietly. 'Our friends are still in there. You have to help them.'

'You could get through in those. Tanks could get through the jungle,' Rupam said.

'They'll get through it all right,' Private Cooper told them. 'That's why they're here. The colonel's got tanks surrounding the village now. But there's no one inside the cordon. He's assured us of that. I don't know where you've come from and you're going to have a lot of explaining to do. But right now I need to get you out of here before the advance begins.'

'What advance?' Ben asked.

'You mean you *are* going into Templeton?' Rupam said.

'*Through* it more like. It's lucky you got out when you did. I don't know what Colonel Greene's got against that village. But pretty soon it'll be nothing but rubble.'

Ben felt cold suddenly. 'What do you mean?'

'He's had it in for that place ever since he spent a week there alone on survival training, a couple of months back. First he had his men vandalise the church – now this.'

'But what is *this*?'

'Colonel Greene's orders. The advance begins in a few hours. We're going to crush that village and everything in it to dust. Let nature take its course.'

Ben gaped in horror. 'But you can't! There are people still in there.'

'You might not even see them if they're indoors or trapped in the jungle,' Rupam added.

'There's no one in there,' Private Cooper told them confidently. 'The whole place has been cleared. Now the village has to be levelled.'

'But why?' Ben demanded. 'Why are you doing this?'

'Colonel's orders. It's an exercise, isn't it?' Private Cooper frowned, as if trying to remember. 'We're doing it because . . . because . . .' His frown deepened. Then his face cleared as he remembered. 'We're training for the landings. Training to flatten a German-occupied village. Destroy it completely and let nature take its course.'

'But can't you see –' Ben started.

He didn't get any further because Private Cooper grabbed him and shoved him towards the waiting Land Rover. Then he pushed Rupam after Ben.

'Right, that's enough now. Let's have a bit of hush and get you to Colonel Greene. Careless talk costs lives, right? And so does breaking into a restricted area. You two are in big trouble.'

Ben stared at Rupam in horror as they were marched up to the Land Rover and bundled in the back.

'Don't you know there's a war on?' Private Cooper said.

11

THE BACK OF THE LAND ROVER WAS CRAMPED and uncomfortable. There was a wooden bench seat running along each side. The tarpaulin that covered the top was rolled up at the back, so at least Ben and Rupam could see out as they bumped across the fields.

'That went well,' Sam said. She was sitting opposite Ben and Rupam.

'Don't start,' Ben told her.

'I didn't say anything,' Rupam protested.

'Sorry. I was just thinking – that went well.'

Ben checked his phone. It still wasn't getting a signal. He stuffed it back in his pocket. His clothes were ripped almost to pieces and he was covered in cuts and scratches. Rupam had fared no better.

'So what now?' Sam asked. She looked as immaculate as ever, of course.

'What do you suggest?' Ben replied.

Rupam shrugged, still assuming that Ben was talking to him. 'We have to convince Colonel Greene to help. You met him – what do you think? Will he listen?'

'No chance,' Sam said. 'You might do better to jump out now and hope no one notices.'

'And hope no one breaks a bone.' Ben sighed. 'Sorry,' he said to Rupam. 'I was just thinking, we could jump out, but it's probably not a good idea. You're right. We need to convince Greene there's a problem. And no, I don't think he'll listen. But we have to try.'

'He knows that Knight and the others are in Templeton. We just need him to hold off the tanks, or use them to mount a rescue mission.'

'But if Growl is right, they have to get to the bottom of what's happening in the village and sort it out. Otherwise those plants and things won't stop at the village. They could spread everywhere.'

The Land Rover was on a narrow track now. It was still bumpy, but not so bad. Sam had shuffled along to the far end of the bench seat and was looking out of the back of the vehicle. Ben moved along to sit opposite.

'What if Colonel Greene won't listen?' Ben

murmured, just loud enough for Sam to hear. 'What if he's infected or whatever as well, and thinks he's training for the D-Day invasion?'

Sam turned to look at him. She replied at normal volume. 'Then we need to get away. Contact Mrs Bailey, Madam Sosostram or someone. There's only so much we can do.' She turned away again. 'That *you* can do,' she corrected herself. 'I'm useless . . . worse than useless. Forget I'm here.'

Private Cooper escorted Ben and Rupam to Colonel Greene's office. Once they were inside the base, there didn't seem much point trying to escape. Even if they got away, they'd be stuck in the middle of a restricted military area anyway. Besides, Rupam was right – their best option was to try to persuade Colonel Greene to help.

Sam walked with them. She said nothing and Ben guessed she was still sulking at not being able to do anything to help.

'It'll be OK,' he told her. 'We'll manage.'

Sam smiled her thanks, but still she said nothing.

'I know,' Rupam said, assuming that Ben was talking to him. But he didn't sound convinced.

The soldier who had come for Ben, Gemma and Knight in the canteen was sitting at his desk in the room outside Colonel Greene's office. Ben remembered his name was Jenkins.

'Are these the children?' Jenkins asked as Cooper led them in.

'No,' Sam said. 'They're a completely different couple of kids who wandered in from a restricted village. What do you think?'

Ben stifled a grin.

'We need to see Colonel Greene,' Rupam said.

Ben could hear the nerves in his voice.

'Oh, you'll see the colonel, all right,' Jenkins told him. He sent Cooper on his way, then turned to Rupam and Ben. 'But he isn't here. You might as well sit down. It could be a while. I doubt you're his absolute number one priority right now. He's got an important training exercise just starting.'

'At Templeton?'

'That's the one. We're going to flatten that place like it never existed.'

'But you can't,' Ben blurted out. 'It won't stop what's happening there. It might just make it worse.'

'I have no idea what you're talking about,' Jenkins said. He sat down at his desk and started working on his computer. 'You should have stayed away, like the colonel told you. He warned you not to go into that village, didn't he?'

Ben looked at Rupam, confused, then back to Jenkins. 'No, he didn't. He knows that Mr Knight and the others are in Templeton.'

'Yeah, nice try.' Jenkins didn't look up from his screen.

'What do you mean?' Rupam asked.

Jenkins looked over at them, irritated. 'Colonel Greene made it very clear that no one was to go anywhere near Templeton. He told me what happened in that meeting. And he told me that he sent Mr Knight and his children away with a flea in their ears and orders to keep well away. Because Templeton is going to be razed to the ground, along with anyone in it.' He pulled his keyboard towards him and started to type. 'So it's a good job you got out when you did. And if there is anyone else there, against the colonel's explicit orders, then I hope you said your goodbyes.'

Ben and Rupam exchanged worried looks, while Sam paced up and down. Rupam had his phone out. He showed Ben that he had no signal.

'That won't work,' Jenkins said, without looking up. 'No mobiles allowed on the base during an operation. We have a suppressor that blanks out any signal. When it's turned on, all mobile phones are dead here.'

'Useless,' Rupam muttered, and put his phone away.

'But *we're* not useless,' Ben said quietly. 'We might think there's nothing we can do, but there is always *something*.'

Sam stopped in front of him, hands on her hips. 'Oh, yeah? What?'

'Sure,' Rupam replied quietly to Ben. 'The question is – what?'

'We do what we're good at. Like remembering things. Or *thinking*.'

Rupam smiled. 'You're the thinker, are you? Genius?'

Ben shook his head. He looked straight at Sam. 'Not me. But that's what we need right now. A thinker. Someone who can come up with a plan, because you're right – we're never going to get Colonel Greene to help.'

'Hey, keep it down, will you?' Jenkins called across. 'Just sit quietly.'

Sam said, 'You won't escape easily from here. Not without a massive distraction.'

Ben nodded. That was true.

'So the only other option is to get a message out. Send for help.'

Ben nodded again. But how?

Sam sighed, as if her next point was obvious. 'So you have to get him out of the room and use the phone.'

She meant Jenkins, of course. But what would make him leave?

'How you do it is up to you,' Sam told Ben. 'I can't be expected to think of everything.'

'I suppose not,' Ben said out loud.

'What?' Rupam said.

Jenkins shot Ben an angry look.

'I said, I suddenly feel very hot,' Ben said quickly. It was actually quite cool in the room. 'I don't feel good at all,' he went on. He pulled off his jacket – scratched to bits by the plants and thorns. 'Oh, that's not good.' He slumped forward, head in his hands. 'Can I get a drink of water? I've not eaten or drunk anything for ages.'

Jenkins came over and looked at Ben.

'He's looking really pale,' Rupam said, guessing Ben was up to something.

'I'm not leaving you to run off,' Jenkins said. 'Nice try, but no chance.'

There was something in his tone – a lack of conviction, an uncertainty that gave Ben hope.

'Please, just some water. Look – lock us in here while you get it if you want. I'll be all right if I can just get a drink . . .' He let his voice tail off weakly.

'There's a water cooler down the hall,' Jenkins said, straightening up. 'I'll be back in one minute, so no funny stuff – right?'

'Funny stuff?' Rupam said as soon as Jenkins was gone. 'Who does he think we are – clowns?'

'Probably,' Sam said.

A key turned in the door. Jenkins was obviously taking no chances.

'That's that, then,' Rupam said. 'Nice try, though.'

'We're not trying to escape,' Ben told him.

'Then what?'

'Phone!'

'He'll be back in a few seconds. We don't have time.'

Rupam was right. Ben dragged Jenkins's heavy desk chair in front of the door and jammed it under the handle.

'Hey, there's a key in Greene's door,' Rupam said. He had pulled open the door to the inner office. 'We can lock ourselves in here.'

'Might buy us a few more minutes,' Ben agreed, running over.

They locked themselves in and jammed one of the upright chairs under the door handle of this room too. Sam was nowhere to be seen. Had she stayed in the other office or just disappeared, Ben wondered?

'So, who do we call?' Rupam asked.

Ben grabbed the phone. 'Gibbet Manor. Someone must be there.'

'Yes, sir?' a voice said at the other end of the phone.

Ben froze. It went through a switchboard. He tried to sound gruff and angry, deepening his voice as best he could. 'Outside line.'

There was a slight pause. Just enough for Ben to know the man on the phone was puzzled. 'Just dial 9, sir.'

'Of course.' Ben hung up. 'Got to dial 9,' he told Rupam.

The door rattled in its frame as someone tried to get in.

'Come on, come on!' Ben muttered into the phone as he waited.

Mrs Bailey answered on the third ring. Ben blurted out as best he could what was happening, but Jenkins was shouting at them through the locked door now.

'Greene's gone mad or something,' Ben finished. 'Don't worry about us, but get Morton to sort it out, to stop the attack. And we'll try to warn Knight and the others.'

'Don't worry,' Mrs Bailey assured him. 'I'm on it. You just look after yourselves. Good luck.'

Ben hardly heard her last words over the sound of splintering wood. The door was breaking as Jenkins forced his way through.

'Come out of there, you little –' Jenkins shouted.

But he was interrupted by another voice: 'All right, Jenkins. You can leave them to me now.'

'Sir?'

'Just get out!' Colonel Greene roared.

Ben and Rupam backed away behind the desk as the door finally crashed open. Colonel Greene stood framed in the broken doorway. He stepped slowly and purposefully into the room.

'You have to call off the exercise,' Ben said. 'There are people in the village. You *know* there are.'

Greene stood the other side of his own desk, staring across at Ben. 'Oh yes, I do know that,' he said quietly.

'Then you'll call it off?' Rupam sounded relieved. 'You'll send the tanks and soldiers in to help?'

'I'm afraid not.'

'But why?' Ben demanded.

Greene leaned forward. His knuckled pressed

down on the desktop as he stared at Ben. His eyes were deep emeralds. He was so close that Ben could see the veins under his skin – like the veins on a leaf. A clump of hairs bristled up through the top of the colonel's collar – like a tuft of grass. Green.

Before Ben really understood what he was seeing, Colonel Greene launched himself across the top of the desk at the two boys. The phone, papers, in-tray – all went flying. Rupam leapt one way, Ben the other.

The colonel's arms were spread wide, grabbing at the two of them, trying to drag them back. Rupam twisted free, but Ben was caught.

'Run!' he yelled at Rupam.

Greene's hand clamped painfully on Ben's upper arm. He struggled and twisted. With his free arm he beat at the colonel, tore at his uniform jacket. A button came away. Then the jacket ripped open.

Rupam ran back, grabbing at Ben and pulling him away. The two of them fell backwards as Ben broke free. They struggled to their feet to see Greene looming over them.

The colonel's jacket was hanging open. His shirt was torn across, leaving a flap of material dangling down. The colonel's chest was bare, his tie was pulled askew.

'Oh, my God,' Rupam said.

Because, under the colonel's shirt, his body was a green mass of twisting tendrils. Creepers and brambles intertwined. Stems and buds trembled with grotesque life. A length of ivy twisted its way up the colonel's neck. He opened his mouth, yelling at Ben and Rupam, and the sound that came out was a guttural snarl of anger. His mouth was bulging with tiny leaves and shoots. His whole body was a writhing tangle of roots and stems and foliage. Soil trickled down as the colonel advanced on Ben and Rupam.

'The Green Man,' Ben gasped in realisation. 'Colonel Greene *is* the Green Man.'

12

RUPAM SEEMED FROZEN TO THE SPOT, STARING at the grotesque form of Colonel Greene. Ben grabbed his friend's hand.

'We have to get out of here!'

Rupam nodded, still unable to look away as Greene started across the room towards them. His hands stretched out. His fingernails were green leaves, tiny spikes growing out like shoots from the tips. Brambles grew up from his back and twisted round his head like a crown of thorns.

Ben dragged Rupam back across the room.

'What the hell is going on?' Jenkins pushed through the splintered door. 'Sir, do you need . . .' He stopped, mid-step, staring past Ben and Rupam.

'Out!' Ben yelled. 'Get out!'

Colonel Greene roared with rage. His cheeks trembled. Leaves and branches swayed in the breeze as he rushed at Ben and Rupam.

Jenkins didn't move. He was right in the path of

the creature bearing down on the boys.

At last, Rupam seemed to switch on. He ran with Ben to the door and they crashed through the shattered remains into the office beyond. Ben risked a quick look back. He wished he hadn't.

Jenkins had not moved. But now he was engulfed in greenery. Branches encircled him, creepers tightening like snakes round his body. A canopy of leaves fell over his head like a wave, knocking him to the ground. From out of the thrashing mass, two emerald-green eyes stared malevolently back at Ben.

The door to the outer office was hanging on its hinges. As he reached the corridor, Ben could hear the sound of running feet.

'We have to get out of here,' he said again. 'We must get back to the village and warn Knight about the assault in case Morton can't stop them.'

'But how?'

Good question, Ben thought. He had no answer. He just ran away from the approaching feet, hoping the corridor led somewhere useful. Anywhere away from Greene and out of the building. He needed fresh air. An open space.

'The soldiers will see what happened,' Ben gasped as they ran.

'They'll stop Greene. Won't they?'

'I don't know. Maybe. Or maybe he'll turn back to normal and blame us for killing Jenkins.'

'Jenkins is dead?' Rupam evidently hadn't looked back.

'I think so. We're all dead if we don't get out of here.'

They ran past offices and closed doors until they reached a staircase. It led down to another corridor and a door – an emergency exit. As soon as Ben pushed the bar to open the door, an alarm sounded.

'Ignore it,' he shouted above the noise.

They were out of the building, close to where the Land Rover had dropped them off. It was still where Private Cooper had parked it what seemed like hours ago.

'Take things slowly,' Rupam said. 'That way we won't look so suspicious.'

It was good advice. Soldiers ran past them, heading for the building they had just left. Several of them looked curiously at the two boys walking the other way. If they'd run, Ben was sure they'd have been stopped. But the soldiers had more important things to deal with right now than a couple of kids who looked as if they were behaving themselves and knew where they were going. If they'd been allowed on to the base, they must have a right to be there.

'Can you drive?' Ben asked as they walked towards the Land Rover.

'Drive? Well, in theory. I know what to do, but I've never tried.'

'Now could be your chance.'

'You're kidding.'

In the distance, several other Land Rovers and a covered army truck were heading along the road that led to the main entrance to the base.

'Could be our only way out,' Ben said.

'I am *so* going to regret this,' Rupam grumbled. 'Why couldn't you have brought Maria? She can drive.'

'She'd complain even more than you. Anyway,' Ben reminded him, 'we didn't have a lot of choice.'

'It's probably locked,' Rupam said when they reached the Land Rover.

It wasn't.

'I bet the keys aren't there,' Rupam said, getting in.

They were.

'They'll stop us at the gate. If we even get that far.'

Ben sighed. 'Oh, for goodness' sake, Rupam! Have you got a better idea?'

He hadn't.

The engine started first time, then stalled as Rupam tried to get the vehicle moving.

'Sorry,' he muttered. 'I can only just reach the pedals.' He found a lever that shifted the seat forward, then tried again.

This time the Land Rover bumped a few metres across the ground before it stopped.

'Try not to attract attention,' Ben said.

'Oh, I'd never have thought of that,' Rupam said. 'Teenage boy driving army Land Rover across a military base. No one will spare us a second thought.'

There was a uniform cap lying on the dashboard in front of Ben. He picked it up and put it on Rupam's head.

'Now they'll think you're a soldier.'

Rupam gave a nervous laugh. 'Let's hope so. A very short soldier.'

Rupam's driving got better and steadier as they crossed the base. Vehicles were still leaving and he was able to position their Land Rover at the back of the line.

'Keep your head down,' Ben suggested. 'That way they can't see your face.'

There didn't seem to be any checks on the convoy leaving the base. All the security was geared towards keeping unauthorised vehicles from getting *in* rather than out. Ben was sure the guards at the main gate would stop them. How could they fail to hear his heart thumping so loudly? How could they miss the fact that Rupam was a kid in a cap and not an army driver?

But they barely glanced at the Land Rover before lowering the barrier behind them.

'Now what?' Rupam said.

'Follow the rest of them till we get close to Templeton.'

'I don't fancy fighting our way back in. Last time was bad enough.'

'I know,' Ben agreed. 'We'll think of something. And we have to go back. We have to warn Knight and the others about Greene.'

Rupam's face was a mask of concentration as he drove. 'You mean warn them that he's sending the tanks in or that he's actually the Green Man of ancient legend?'

'Both, I suppose. How can he be, though?' Ben said. 'How can Colonel Greene be the Green Man? What we saw – it's impossible.'

'Evidently not,' Rupam said. 'Maybe Growl can explain it. A man made of plants and stuff – I agree, it's . . . strange.'

'Have you ever heard of anything like it?'

Rupam shook his head. The cap was too big for him and it started sliding on his head. He pulled it off and tossed it into the back of the vehicle. 'Have you?'

'Well,' Ben said, 'at the home there was this guy who used to deliver to the kitchens. He brought potatoes and carrots and cabbage – things like that. We called him the Vegetable Man.'

Rupam glanced at Ben before looking back at the road ahead. His mouth curled into a smile. Then he laughed. Ben laughed too. The Land Rover lurched and bumped as they both laughed away some of their tension and fear.

The convoy was moving faster than Rupam was happy to drive. It slowly disappeared into the distance, which Ben thought was probably a good thing.

'We don't want to end up parked by the tanks and army lorries. We'll just get caught and hauled back to face Greene.'

'You really think he'll get away with it?' Rupam asked.

'Either he's behind all this or he's somehow been infected and taken over. Whichever it is, if the soldiers can believe it's 1943, then they can be convinced their commanding officer isn't a crazy, violent plant monster.'

'I suppose,' Rupam agreed.

Ahead of them, the road forked. Ben could see the convoy in the distance on the left.

'Go right,' he told Rupam.

'Will this take us back towards Templeton?'

'We'll need to turn left further on, I think.'

They drove for several miles before they found a left turn. The Land Rover bumped along the narrow lane, hedges rising on either side.

'Do you think we're safe?' Ben wondered.

'Who knows? The closer we get to the village, the more likely we are to run into trouble. Soon we'll reach the barrier. What do we do then?'

The narrow lane ended at another junction. They turned right on to a wider road, which Rupam recognised as the one they'd taken into the village when they first arrived here with Madam Sosostram.

'Are you sure?' Ben asked. The roads all looked pretty much the same to him – fields on one side and a high hedge on the other. 'No, don't answer that. Of course you're sure.'

'I remember it exactly,' Rupam said. 'The roadblock is round the next bend.'

He slowed the Land Rover and they edged cautiously forward. But the army roadblock had gone.

'Joined the main advance, maybe,' Ben suggested.

Before long they reached the barrier, which for all the world was like a massive hedge growing across the road. But a hedge that could snare and kill them, Ben knew.

Rupam stopped the Land Rover. 'What now?'

'Is it the same as it was before?' Ben had the beginnings of an idea. 'Exactly the same?'

'Well, not exactly. It's grown, but it doesn't seem to have moved any further from the village. It looks pretty much the same.'

'There.' Ben pointed. 'That's where we got through before, isn't it? Where you hacked a path with the sword?'

'Yes. You can see where the foliage is a bit thinner. It hasn't grown back fully.'

'Then that's where we aim for,' Ben decided. 'The weakest point.'

'Hang on.' Rupam was looking worried. 'What do you mean, "aim for"? We don't have the sword any more. We'll never force our way through again.'

'Not on foot,' Ben agreed. 'But we're in a Land Rover.'

Rupam's jaw dropped. 'Oh, come on! You're not suggesting . . .' He looked from Ben to the mass of foliage and back again. 'Are you? You're crazy!'

'We have to get through,' Ben insisted.

Rupam shook his head. 'I must be crazy too,' he decided. 'Make sure your seat belt's on and hold tight.'

The engine roared and the Land Rover gathered speed as it hurtled towards the wall of green. It smashed into the foliage at the exact point where Ben and Rupam had forced their way through before.

The windscreen was suddenly dark – plastered with leaves. Branches slashed at the side windows and scraped along the paintwork. The whole vehicle shook. Rupam kept his foot hard down on the accelerator.

The wheels bounced over roots and creepers. The whole vehicle lifted in the air as it hit a large obstacle. The bonnet slammed down. Metal screeched and protested. The windscreen shattered, showering Ben and Rupam in broken glass.

They were slowing. A fist of ivy and bramble punched in through the window beside Ben, ripping the seat covering. It was whipped away as the vehicle kept going. But they were losing speed. The Land Rover slewed sideways as a tyre burst. Ben could hear rubber flapping against metal.

Ahead, he thought he could see the merest hint of daylight. The vehicle shuddered and slowed. It then tilted, skidded back the other way and stopped. The bonnet was once more facing forward. Behind them, Ben could dimly see a trail of broken branches and scattered leaves. In front of them, the leaves closed in, rustling in what sounded like anticipation.

Rupam thumped at the steering wheel, cursing under his breath. The engine was protesting and the vehicle rocked as Rupam tried to get it moving again – and failed.

They were trapped inside the Land Rover, so close to the end of the barrier of greenery that Ben thought he could see the outline of the road beyond. Branches pressed in from the sides. The green wall in front reared up, gathering itself ready to pour through the broken windscreen and tear the two boys to pieces.

13

THE SEAT BELT WAS JAMMED. BEN STRUGGLED to unclick it, twisting desperately out of the way of the advancing plants. Finally, he managed, hurling himself sideways as a shaft of wood rammed into the back of the seat where he had been.

'Out!' Rupam yelled. 'We have to get out!'

The doors were held shut by the weight of the foliage outside. The only other exits were via the back of the Land Rover or through the broken windscreen.

'Windscreen,' Ben decided. At least they'd be heading in the right direction and he still thought he could see a glimmer of light ahead of them.

Together they dived out on to the bonnet of the vehicle. Leaves whipped at them and branches lashed out. They pushed their way through as best they could, crawling and sliding across the front of the Land Rover, then falling into the barbed greenery below.

They crawled onwards, thorns and undergrowth clawing and tearing at them. Rupam crashed to the ground, his leg tangled in a creeper that dragged him backwards. He grabbed at Ben, who tried to hold on but lost his grip. Desperately, Ben reached back, grabbing Rupam again. This time he was able to keep hold, ripping his friend clear of the danger.

With a final, frantic burst of energy, they scrabbled forward. Daylight replaced the olive green that had lit their world. Ben could taste the fresh air. He hadn't realised how cloying and close the various scents of the plants were until he was free of them. He rolled and tumbled out of the thrashing foliage and on to the hard tarmac of the road.

At once he was on his feet, gripping Rupam's flailing arms and dragging him clear too.

'Thanks,' Rupam gasped. 'I thought we'd had it.'

Ben looked back at the wall of green. It was bulging out towards them. Stems curled and budded, extended and grew towards them at an alarming rate.

'Let's get out of here,' he said. 'We must find Gemma, Knight and the others.'

Even the grass was their enemy. Rupam stepped off the roadway on to the verge and was at once under attack. The grass curled up over his feet, growing rapidly and wrapping itself round his shoe, threading into it. He tore himself free and jumped back into the road.

The hedges either side bristled and moved as the boys passed, as if caught in a gale. Except there wasn't even a breeze. Branches of a nearby horse chestnut tree dipped down towards them. Ivy snaked across the road as if it was being pulled by some invisible hand.

'How long before the plants overrun the place, do you think?' Rupam asked.

'No idea. Webby's probably watching on the satellite. He'll know.'

'He'll see the tanks,' Rupam said. 'I wonder if Captain Morton has managed to get Greene to stop the advance.'

Neither of them thought Greene could be stopped easily. They walked on in brooding silence. Soon the broken top of the church tower became visible over the swaying hedges. At last they were within sight of the centre of the village. It looked very different from the last time they had seen it.

It was as if the clock had been wound forward fifty years. The grass at the side of the road was longer and thicker. The shells of the buildings were almost invisible beneath layers of ivy and creeper. The front of the pub was covered with wisteria, gnarled branches digging into the stonework and winding through the broken windows. The phone box was almost lost in a dense shroud of green.

'Where is everyone?' Ben wondered.

'I don't even see any ghosts.' Rupam checked his phone. 'No, nothing.'

'The church was the centre of things,' Ben remembered from the satellite pictures. It made him think of the basement of Gibbet Manor, of watching the computer images. 'Do you think Webby smells?'

'What?' Rupam was momentarily confused by the sudden change of subject. 'Of course he smells. Stuck down in a cellar all day, never coming out even to take a bath. You'd smell.'

'I suppose.' Ben wanted to point out that he didn't think it was that sort of smell.

'Can we get through the graveyard?' Rupam asked. 'The path was rather overgrown.'

They walked warily past a large oak tree, its branches and leaves rustling ominously. It was on a raised patch of green behind a low stone wall. Both of them watched it carefully as they walked by. But the threat came from another direction.

Ivy was growing along the low wall, forcing its way through the gaps between the stones and clawing into the mortar. The wall was now held up only by the latticework of ivy and creepers. Ben was so intent on the tree that he didn't notice the ivy twitching as he and Rupam walked past. Didn't see the leaves curling and the stems straining back from the stonework. Coiling. Tensing.

Suddenly, the whole wall exploded. The ivy and brambles and bindweed that covered it lashed out, bringing chunks of stone and cement with them. A hailstorm of masonry whipped past Ben and Rupam. A large stone ripped from the wall caught Rupam on the shoulder, making him cry out. More followed, catapulted by the thrashing plants.

The web of interlaced ivy and creepers was a wall itself, lunging for the boys. A canopy of green crashed down on them, blotting out the sky.

Ben grabbed Rupam and hurled him to the ground, crawling rapidly away from under the ivy. But it was wrapping itself round his legs, tightening on his throat. Rupam too was gasping for breath, clawing at the wiry green that ensnared him, throttling him.

The foliage creaked and hissed as it tore at them. But then there was another sound – the ring of metal connecting with the wood and leaves. The rasp of a sword against the binding weeds and plants.

Maria was silhouetted against the pale sky. She hacked down, twisted the sword and slashed again and again at the greenery that held Ben and Rupam tight.

The ivy shrank away. Creepers broke and fell under Maria's expert cuts. Ben managed to crawl out from beneath the canopy. Rupam followed close behind him. He tore a length of ivy from his neck and threw it back into the mass of greenery.

'Thanks,' he gasped to Maria.

'Don't thank me yet. We need to get back into the pub.'

'Why the pub?' Rupam asked hoarsely as they ran for the door.

'Only building still structurally sound enough to keep out the plants. We can't stay in the open and it's closer than the church.' Maria stopped clear of the door. 'I'll go first. You guys stay close on my heels, OK?'

They didn't need to ask why. The wisteria had closed like a curtain across the open doorway, barring the entrance.

Maria raised her sword and cried, 'Ready?' Then she ran straight at the covered doorway, slashing and cutting at the thick stems. She hardly slowed, diving through the narrowest of gaps before the plant could close in again.

Rupam was right behind her, with Ben on his heels. The branches grabbed at Ben as he dived through after the others. He felt his jacket snag and rip, but he kept going, tumbling into the pub.

It was almost dark – the windows were covered with foliage. A few candles gave what little light there was. Enough to see Knight and Growl standing at the dusty bar, and Gemma sitting on one of the few remaining chairs.

'Glad you could join us,' Knight said. His suit was torn and stained. 'Though I don't think we'll be staying here long. It's only a matter of time before it breaks in through the windows and the door.'

'I imagine it thinks we are less of a threat cooped up in here,' Growl said. 'So we must prove how wrong that assumption is.'

'We lost the research notes and documents in the school,' Maria told them. She was standing by the door, sword at the ready. 'What can we do if we don't even know what's really going on here?'

'But we do know,' Rupam blurted out. 'That's why we came back – well, partly. We had to warn you.'

'Warn us about what?' Knight demanded.

'About Colonel Greene,' Ben said. 'He's not just crazy – he's the Green Man.'

The others listened in astonished silence as Ben and Rupam took turns to explain and recount their adventures.

'We got a message through to Mrs Bailey,' Ben finished. 'She is going to ask Captain Morton to stop the tanks.'

'But why stop them?' Gemma said. 'If they're going to destroy all this, won't that sort everything out?'

'Not if Greene really is an embodiment of the ancient earth gods,' Growl told her sharply. 'Don't you listen to anything?' His lip curled in sudden anger. 'The village itself, or something here in it, is the only thing holding back the power of the Green Man. Keeping it in check, as it always has done – perhaps right back to pagan times. It's that power that has stopped the green from radiating out even further. It's like the force of gravity, holding it in. If that *gravity* is destroyed, if Colonel Greene manages to get rid of that *inhibitor*, whatever it is, then the Green Man will be free to escape from the village and spread his malign influence everywhere.'

Ben had been about to interrupt – to tell Growl he was being unfair to Gemma. But Knight was watching closely and saw Ben's irritation. He caught his eye and shook his head, telling Ben to stay silent.

'It's bad, isn't it?' Knight said to Growl as the clergyman fell silent.

There was a sheen of sweat across Growl's brow. He nodded. 'I'm sorry, Gemma,' he murmured, but the words seemed an effort.

'Then it's getting stronger. It senses something is about to happen. The powers here are building. If what you say is right, then Greene's plan is to destroy the village in order to get rid of this inhibitor. In effect, to free himself – the Green Man, the malign forces of nature – to escape from this area and spread out far and wide.' Knight turned to Maria. 'You ready to get us out of here?'

She nodded. 'But where will we go? The plants are everywhere.'

'The church is the centre of it all,' Growl said. He was breathing heavily, as if trying to control a panic attack. 'And it's the oldest building. It must be something to do with the church.'

'The foliate heads?' Rupam asked. 'The representations of the Green Man on the tower.'

'Perhaps, perhaps. I need time to think.' Growl dabbed at his forehead with a grubby handkerchief.

'You all right?' Ben asked Gemma quietly.

She nodded. 'He gets like that. It's OK. I don't mind.'

He could tell that she did mind – the girl was still pale from Growl's verbal onslaught. Ben knew from his own experience that the clergyman was given to sudden angry outbursts, usually when the situation was dire.

'At least the ghosts have gone,' Ben said.

She forced a smile. 'Most of them. The ones that aren't here always, anyway.'

'That's what I meant.'

Gemma stood up from her chair. She put her hand on Ben's shoulder and spoke quietly, close to his ear. 'I know.'

'Know? Know what?'

Somehow, Sam was sitting on the chair where Gemma had just been. 'Oh, come on, Ben,' she said. 'She's always known. Right from the start.'

'I know,' Gemma said quietly, 'that you can't see the ghosts and demons. Not without your phone.'

'The only mystery,' Sam said, inspecting her nails, 'is why she doesn't tell Knight and the others that Ben Foundling is a fraud and a liar.' She looked up at Ben. 'Don't you think?'

'Don't worry. I won't tell anyone,' Gemma said, oblivious to Sam's words.

'But why not?'

She shrugged. 'I can see enough ghosts for both of us.'

Ben wanted to ask her more, to get her to explain. But the others were ready to leave now. The plants were hammering insistently against the windows, as if preparing to attack. The doorway bulged with green and brown stems, shoots, leaves . . .

And from away in the distance, over the sound of the thrashing plants, came another sound: a low rumbling like thunder, only more constant, more insistent, more mechanical . . . Engines.

'The tanks are coming,' Ben realised. 'Greene's started the advance.'

14

'THE CHURCH,' GROWL DECIDED. 'THAT WAS THE focal point until the Puritans destroyed the statues. That was where the power of the Green Man was held in check. Something there must still be holding Greene back. It all centres on the church, so that is where we will find answers and where we must make for.'

'If we can get out of here,' Ben muttered.

'Can we jump from upstairs?' Rupam asked. He was having to talk loudly to be heard above the thrashing of the plants and the rumble of the tanks. 'Like we managed to climb over the plants at the school?'

'There are no stairs,' Knight told them. 'They've collapsed.'

Overhead, the ceiling creaked ominously.

'Sounds like we're too late anyway,' Growl added. 'It's probably got in through the windows.'

'Only one thing for it, then,' Maria decided, raising her sword.

'She's good with that,' Sam said quietly in Ben's ear.

'But is she good enough?' he murmured back. He glanced round, but Sam had gone.

'You ready?' Maria said.

Gemma nodded nervously, biting her lip. Rupam and Ben braced themselves, prepared to run.

'I don't think we have any option,' Knight admitted.

'Just get on with it, girl,' Growl said, his voice hard-edged again and his brow beaded with sweat.

Maria was a blur of motion. The sword spun and sliced, hacking and cutting at the green curtain across the doorway. The plants drew back, almost as if they were surprised by the sudden onslaught.

Knight pushed the boys and Gemma after Maria. He and Growl followed. The vegetation across the doorway was not thick and already Maria was slicing through to the daylight beyond. She stepped out on to the street, the sun behind her so that she was silhouetted – the sword raised above her head, poised and ready.

Ben forced his way through the gap. Stems and leaves whipped at him as he went, as the plants tried to close in again. He staggered out after Rupam and Gemma, and turned to see Knight and Growl struggle through the foliage and emerge into the road.

'You mentioned some inhibitor, a focus for the energy that has held the plants in check,' Knight said. He was breathing heavily as he spoke to Growl.

The clergyman nodded. 'Something in or close to the church, I would guess.'

'In the graveyard?' Knight said. 'In a grave?'

Growl raised his hand to stop him. 'Yes,' he breathed. 'Yes, that could very well be. You are thinking of the grave of the Memento Mori knight?'

'I am.'

'All the more reason to get to the church,' Ben told them.

They kept to the middle of the road. The grass on the verges quivered and twisted as they passed. Branches dipped and swung from the trees. If any got dangerously close, Maria hacked at them with her sword.

'Do you think the Memento Mori knight buried in the churchyard is there because of . . .' Ben wasn't sure how to describe thing. He gestured vaguely at the world in general. 'Because of all this?'

'Unfinished business,' Rupam added. 'That's why they buried them aligned north–south, you said.'

Growl nodded. 'Think back to the role of the Memento Mori in recent events, what we know about the order, and think about the name of this place.'

'I don't follow,' Ben admitted. 'The only thing I know about the Memento Mori is that they stopped that Gabriel Diablo bloke hundreds of years ago.'

Growl turned and fixed Ben with a piercing stare. 'Exactly.'

'The Temple of the Holy Crystal,' Rupam remembered. 'That's what the village is named after, remember? The Memento Mori temple.'

Knight was frowning at Growl. 'Are you serious? Diablo's *Crystal* – here?'

'Why not? One of the fabled artefacts that has been lost for centuries. We know that the Memento Mori took it and we know that here they founded a Temple of the Holy *Crystal*.'

'And the Crystal was created by Diablo as some sort of focusing device for his power,' Knight said. 'That could fit.'

'But why are things happening right now?' Maria asked, cutting casually through a trailing branch of cedar.

'The ceremony that Carstairs Endeavour held to summon Mortagula,' Knight said. 'Could that have somehow activated or interfered with the other artefacts – the ones he didn't have?'

'I have no idea, but anything is possible,' Growl told him. 'Now, please let's stop speculating and try to discover the truth. When we get to the church, let's hope we can find answers to all these questions.'

'If we ever get there,' Ben said.

Even as he said it, there was the sound of a muffled thud, followed moments later by an explosion. A cloud of smoke and dust rose above the hedge to the side of the road.

It was followed almost at once by a similar sound. Another explosion, close to the first. Grit and mud blasted past Ben and the others.

'They're shelling the village,' Knight shouted above the noise. 'They're going to level it completely.'

The road ahead exploded. Chunks of tarmac flew at them, rising dust blotting out the light. The rumble of the tanks was getting louder all the time, approaching from behind.

'We have to stop them,' Growl yelled. 'The Crystal – if it is the Crystal – is barely holding the Green Man in check now. If the tanks destroy it, we have no hope!'

They were level with a ruined house set back from the road. Honeysuckle and climbing roses formed a latticework over the broken walls. The roof had gone and the windows were empty sockets. Everyone turned towards the house as they heard the sound of a powerful engine from the other side of it.

Moments later, a tank ploughed through the building. The gun appeared first, then the main body of the heavy vehicle shattered through the stonework, sending debris flying. The front of the tank lurched upwards as it climbed the remains of the house wall. Then it slammed down, bricks and stone crunching under the tracks.

'Get to the church,' Knight yelled at Growl. Then he turned to the others. 'All of you, get to the church.' He grabbed the nearest person by the shoulder – it was Ben. 'Not you. You can help me here.'

'Help you do *what*?' Ben shouted back.

The tank was heaving through the remains of the building. A side wall collapsed behind it. The vehicle turned, one track stopping as the other kept going to line it up with the roadway. Then it lurched forward again.

'We're going to talk to the crew of that tank. Find out if there's any way to stop the attack.'

The tank slammed down on to the roadway, just metres from where Ben and Knight were standing. They dashed out of the way. Knight jumped on to the grass verge and from there up on to the broken remains of the wall of the house. As the tank rumbled past, he leapt on to the back of it.

Ben was not so fast. The tank was already pulling away, too far from him. If he tried to jump on now, he'd get caught in the tracks at the back. He ran along the broken wall, parts of which were only a few bricks high. He could feel the masonry crumbling under his feet.

Knight reached for Ben from the back of the tank. He was holding on to a part of the metalwork with one hand, stretching with the other as far as he could to grab Ben.

'Jump!' Knight yelled, though Ben couldn't hear him above the straining roar of the engine. Black exhaust blasted out.

He leapt. Ben was still running as he left the ground. The fumes stung the back of his throat. His hand brushed against Knight's, but he couldn't hold on. He was falling.

Frantically, Ben flailed his arms, trying to balance on the sloping back of the tank. He was perched on a curving section that covered the top of the tracks. If he fell . . .

A hand grabbed his wrist and dragged him away from the edge.

'Thanks,' Ben gasped. 'Now what?' He doubted Knight could hear him.

It was hard to stay upright as the tank lurched and bumped along the road. They were shaken to their knees as it skirted the hole in the road caused by the shelling. The tank slowed, the gun raising slightly. There was a huge rush of noise as it fired. Ben could hear the whine of the shell.

In the distance, the wall of a ruined house exploded into fragments.

With the tank still going more slowly, Knight leapt up on to the turret. He gestured urgently for Ben to follow. Hoping the turret wasn't about to turn and throw him off, Ben clambered up after Knight.

There was a heavy, circular hatch on top of the tank. Ben guessed it could be sealed from the inside, but although it was shut, it was bouncing in its frame as the tank moved. Knight grabbed at an external handle and heaved it open. Ben helped him fold it back so that it lay flat across the turret.

'Why didn't they lock it?' he shouted.

Knight was staring down into the tank. When he looked across at Ben, his face was pale. 'Because someone was trying to get out,' he shouted back. 'Maybe all of them were. Let's hope they made it.'

Ben leaned forward to look down through the hatch – to see what had made Knight turn pale.

The inside of the tank was dimly lit by internal lights. The sunlight shone down through the hatch, giving further illumination. He could make out the vague shapes of the crew, the metal sides of the cabin, the first aid box marked with a white cross and the word 'Emergency' fixed to the inside of the turret . . . It took Ben several moments to realise what he was really looking at.

'There's no one here,' he finally said out loud.

Or was there? As he leaned in through the hatch, his eyes adjusted and he could make out more details. The whole interior was smothered with branches and leaves. Gnarled wood jutted through the leaves, curving round the tank's controls. Ivy and creepers laced through the systems and the gun.

But it wasn't a disorderly mass of vegetation like the creeping hedges. There was purpose to it. The greenery was *driving* the tank, firing its gun. The sinewy branches, thick trunks, tendrils and leaves were very definite shapes. They looked at first glance like *people*. That was why it had taken Ben a moment to work out what he was seeing.

A section of leaves turned as if to look at Ben as he stared down into the tank. The way they were arranged, the way the veins ran across them and the stems linked them together, the leaves could almost be a face.

Could *have been* a face.

'I was wrong. The crew didn't get out,' Knight was shouting to Ben. 'They didn't have time.'

Ben could see exactly what Knight meant even before the man said it.

'They've been taken over, possessed. Probably when the tank came through those hedges surrounding the village. They've become plant life. Just like the Green Man.'

15

THE INSIDE OF THE TANK WAS ALIVE. LIKE A single creature, the foliage and greenery, the branches and leaves, swung round towards the open hatch. Faster than Ben could have imagined, a length of branch shot upwards, stabbing towards him.

He tried to move, lost his balance and fell. The tank lurched beneath him. The branch disappeared back inside as the tank crashed through a low wall and tore across the grass. Ben was jolted forward, falling. He reached out his arms to stop himself tumbling inside the tank, into the greenery. His right hand connected painfully with the first aid box, knocking the clasp. As the box fell open, bandages and tubes of cream and field dressings fell out.

And something else. Ben's scrabbling hand closed on something cold and metallic. Instinctively he grabbed it – a gun.

Then he felt strong hands on his shoulders, heaving him back up and out of the hatch. Knight pulled him clear and they both fell backwards – just as a mass of ivy poured out of the hatch, like water boiling over on a stove.

The gun was chunky and crude, with a very wide barrel. Ben hadn't seen anything like it before. It looked more like an old toy than a real gun.

'Flare pistol,' Knight shouted above the noise of the engine. 'Might be useful to signal for help. Only one shot, though, so let's not waste it.'

Ben stuffed the flare pistol into the pocket of his ragged jacket.

'Now what?' he yelled back.

The ivy was still boiling out of the hatch, trailing towards them. It coiled and writhed, dragging itself forward.

'Nothing we can do here. Time we were going,' Knight decided. 'We'll have to jump for it.'

He took Ben's hand and together they leapt from the moving vehicle. The impact of their landing shook Ben's hand out of Knight's. He rolled and tumbled. The tank wasn't moving fast, but it was a long way down. The grass beneath Ben was pulling at him like Velcro, hooking into his clothes and tearing at his skin.

Ben staggered to his feet and ran for the nearest safety – the narrow road the tank was still rumbling along.

'It's heading out of the village again,' Knight said, joining Ben. His face was scratched and his jacket was in shreds. 'Taking the curse of the Green Man, or whatever you want to call it, on to pastures new. We have to stop this before it spreads too far.'

The shelling hadn't stopped. The noise of the tank had simply deadened the sound of the explosions in the village. Some small areas of vegetation had been hit and were burning, but the tanks were aiming at the buildings not the jungle. Smoke rose above the swaying trees, turning the sky to a gunmetal grey. The already ruined buildings were little more than piles of rubble. There was only one structure still standing high enough for Ben to see it properly.

'Why haven't they been shooting at the church tower?' he said.

'I was just wondering the same thing,' Knight said. 'I think we should find out.'

Getting to the church was a nightmare. The entire landscape was coming to life. The grass under Ben's feet clawed and tore at him. The trees and bushes lashed out as he passed. Branches whipped at his face, while creepers and tendrils fought to ensnare him.

They kept to open ground as much as they could, not daring to pause for breath or even slow down as they ran for the distant tower that stood proud and defiant against the smoke-filled sky.

The churchyard was a wasteland of ragged tombstones and writhing, overgrown grass. Ben pushed through the broken remains of a wall. Knight, who was close behind him, paused to rip brambles away before they could grab him.

Ben braced himself, then charged into a tangle of undergrowth. His foot twisted awkwardly on a lump of stone buried in the thrashing grass and weeds. Knight arrived beside him, also stumbling and grabbing Ben's shoulder for support.

'From the wall,' Knight said, kicking at a large piece of pale stone.

They waded through the clawing vegetation, tearing free of the clutching grass.

'*That's* not from the wall,' Ben said.

Half buried in the churning grass was a head. A head carved from stone. The chipped, weathered face stared up at Ben through blank eyes. One side of it had been smashed away – recently, since the stone here was pale and unblemished.

'There's more,' Knight said.

He was right. Ben could now see a fractured body – part of the same statue or a different one? Another broken head, lying beside a mossy gravestone . . . A section of leg . . . An arm poking up like a pale branch . . .

A head and shoulders stuck out from the ground further on. The crucifix was still just discernible at the figure's ancient neck.

'I think we found where the Puritans dumped the statues of the saints after they smashed them,' Knight said.

A shout from further into the churchyard drew their attention. Maria was standing with her sword raised. She waved it to attract their attention, the blade gleaming.

'Over here,' she called.

She then ran towards them, hacking aside the brambles and tangled grass that tried to impede her progress. She forged a path they could follow back to where Gemma was standing beside a large pile of dark earth.

'We found the Memento Mori grave,' Gemma told Knight as he and Ben joined the others.

Growl was digging with a short-handled spade. The edge of the blade had rusted away, but despite the earlier rain the ground was dry and powdery. He had dug deep, standing in a pit almost up to his shoulders. Rupam was working with him, scraping away loose soil in a metal fire bucket and chucking it up on to a growing pile above.

Maria stood ready with the sword, constantly watching for any movement from the plants and undergrowth round them.

'Enough,' Growl told Rupam. He leaned his spade against the steep side of the pit and scrabbled at the floor with his bare hands. 'I think this is it.' He looked up for a moment at Knight, Ben and Gemma, who were all staring down into the pit. 'The coffin has decayed, of course. We found a few splinters of wood. Fragments, nothing more. But this . . .'

Growl teased something pale from the earth with his fingers. It was a human skull. The jaw was missing and it was stained with age.

'There's this too,' Rupam said. He had found the broken hilt of a sword.

'Memento Mori,' Knight said. 'Anything else? Any sign of the Crystal?'

Growl carefully replaced the skull where he had

found it. He took the remains of the sword from Rupam and laid that down too.

Rupam gave a sudden yell, leaping back as Maria's sword flashed through the air towards him. But he was not the target. A sinewy root broke out from the earth at the side of the grave pit, stabbing towards him. The sword cut through it easily and the root fell to the bottom of the grave. It twitched for a moment, then was still.

Growl seemed not to have noticed. He had found something else. It looked like a pouch or a small bag made of dark leather. It was torn and scuffed and falling to pieces. And in the muted light of the pit, it seemed to be glowing.

'The Crystal?' Ben wondered.

'Open it,' Gemma urged.

Growl tipped the small bag up, emptying it into the palm of his hand. In among the loose soil and torn bits of the bag's lining, something burned with a pale white light. Growl let the soil and debris scatter through his fingers. He was left with an object about the size of a golf ball, but faceted and gleaming with inner luminescence.

'Holy Crystal!' Maria said.

'Indeed,' Growl told her. He held it up between his thumb and forefinger, gazing deep into the glowing heart. Then he let it fall into his palm and tossed it up to Knight.

'Diablo's Crystal,' Knight agreed.

'It's glowing,' Ben said. 'Does that mean it's working? That it's doing whatever it's supposed to be doing?'

'In that case, why are the plants going wild?' Rupam asked, clambering out of the pit, then reaching down to help Growl scramble up after him.

'A good question, young man,' Growl said.

They all stared in fascination at the Crystal now resting in Knight's palm. Sam leaned forward, her hand on Ben's shoulder, to get a better look.

'I wish you wouldn't do that,' he murmured.

'Sorry,' she said out loud. 'Would you rather I wasn't here?'

'You're not,' he *almost* said.

'Have you told Growl about the saints?' Sam asked. She obviously knew he hadn't. 'Tell him about the saints.'

'What about the saints?' Ben asked her, more loudly than he had intended.

'What saints?' Growl asked.

'Oh, yes,' said Knight, slipping the glowing Crystal into his jacket pocket. 'Probably not important, but it might interest you to know that we stumbled – literally – over the broken-up statues from the church tower.'

Growl frowned. 'Where?'

Ben pointed. 'Over there. Only . . .' There was something in the back of his mind that wasn't right. He tried to remember exactly how the broken stones had looked.

'But if they were removed hundreds of years ago,' Gemma said, 'how come they're still here? Wouldn't someone have taken them away by now?'

That was it. 'They weren't though, were they?' He remembered the clean, new break down the side of one of the heads. 'It's recent. It has to be. That's why this is all happening now, isn't it?'

Sam was nodding. 'Has to be,' she agreed, though no one else heard her.

'If the statues were recently moved, their spell over the Green Man was broken,' Growl said, thinking it through. 'The Crystal alone isn't enough to keep everything in check. But who removed the statues and why?'

'Greene,' Ben realised. 'When we got through the barrier, one of the soldiers said something about Greene vandalising the church.' He turned to Rupam. 'What did he say exactly? Do you remember?'

Rupam nodded. 'Of course. He said . . .' The boy stared thoughtfully into the distance as he recalled the conversation. 'He said, "I don't know what Colonel Greene's got against that village. But pretty soon it'll be nothing but rubble . . ." Then Ben asked what he meant and he said, "He's had it in for that place ever since he spent a week there alone on survival training, a couple of months back. First he had his men vandalise the church – now this."'

'"This" meaning the tanks,' Ben explained. 'And vandalising the church – that must be it. Didn't he tell us he'd camped out in the churchyard or something?'

'If Greene was here, in the churchyard for a while, he might have been infected. Possessed,' Knight said.

Growl nodded. 'If he was susceptible. His name suggests an ancestral link of some sort to the ancient priests and elders who worshipped the Green Man. And so the Green Man was presented with someone he could use to remove the blocks on his power. Despite those blocks, he managed to get inside Greene's mind and persuade him to remove the statues and break them up. To start the process of setting him free. With every statue Greene broke up, the power over him grew . . .'

'We can hardly put the broken statues back together again,' Maria pointed out.

'But we can destroy the church tower,' Growl told them. 'It used to be the force that held the Green Man back, when the statues of the saints were intact. Now it's become a symbol of his supremacy and his freedom now the statues have gone.'

'Which is why the tanks are not firing on it,' Ben realised.

'Destroying the rest of the village,' Knight agreed. 'Returning that to nature, but preserving its own source of power and influence.'

His words were punctuated by the distant thunder of an explosion.

'It won't take them much longer,' Gemma said.

'And then the tanks will roll out of the village and keep going, taking the Green Man with them,' Ben said. 'Nowhere will be safe.' In his mind's eye he could see again the horrifying contents of the tank – a weapon of destruction driven by a force of nature . . .

'The natives are getting restless,' Maria said.

All around them the grass was twisting and leaning as if in a breeze. Trees swayed and thrashed.

'To the tower,' Growl ordered. 'Quickly.'

'But how can we destroy a church tower?' Ben asked.

His words were lost in the noise all around them.

'It knows what we're saying, what we're planning,' Knight shouted. 'How can that be?'

Growl shook his head. 'It senses something, certainly. We must hurry.'

Together they ran towards the tower. It was like running into the wind while wading through deep water. The tower was dark and forbidding, rising up over the churchyard. The church itself looked small and fragile by comparison.

Maria hacked her way through the thickening jungle of plants. Ben and the others forced their way through after her. The sound of the approaching tanks grew louder and closer with every second that passed.

Ben was near enough now to see the alcoves in the sides of the tower, where the statues of the saints had stood. The carved foliate heads – the representations of the Green Man – were still there. Hideous, misshapen faces stared out from the midst of carved wreaths of foliage. Blank eyes watched sightlessly from a mass of leaves and stems, stained green by the damp years.

Except that the eyes were not blank or sightless. They were intent, staring at Ben and his friends with malevolent life. The faces looked down on them, snarling in rage – just like the face Ben had seen inside the tank.

16

THE WALL OF FOLIAGE WAS BULGING AGAIN. The noise was deafening. A huge battle tank tore through the undergrowth, its tracks shredding grass and branches.

Ben was standing right in front of it, frozen to the spot. He felt someone grab his shoulders and drag him away. The two of them fell, the tank crashing past just a metre away. He saw Gemma and Rupam leaping for cover on the other side. Growl and Knight were also rolling clear. Twisting round, Ben saw with surprise that it was Maria who had saved him.

She got to her feet and retrieved her fallen sword. 'Don't mention it,' she yelled above the sound of the disappearing tank.

There was a massive straggly hedge around them. No sign of the others.

'It's trying to keep us from the tower,' Ben said. 'Oh, and yes – thanks.'

Maria forced a quick smile. 'We need to get back to the others. There's no way we can destroy the church tower on our own.'

'There's no way we can destroy the church tower full stop,' Ben told her.

But he didn't know if she heard. Maria was swinging the sword in a wide arc, lopping off the ends of plants, hacking through branches. The narrow leaves of a weeping willow dipped towards them. Maria's sword sent them spinning away like green confetti.

The whole landscape had changed as the mass of vegetation moved in. It was difficult to tell even where the tower was any more. The trees arched above Ben and Maria, so it seemed as if they were in a vast green cathedral.

They backed away towards the gap where the tank had driven through. Already it was closing up, like green doors sliding unevenly across. Above the constant rustle of the plants, Ben could hear the distant crump of explosions and the rumbling of the tanks. Beyond that he thought he could hear someone shouting – Rupam? Knight?

'Come on,' Ben cried.

He could think of only one way to demolish the church tower. Only one way to bring a halt to this whole business – assuming Growl was right.

Maria backed away from the encroaching plants, sword poised.

'Where are we going?' she asked.

'We're following that tank.'

She spun on her heel to swipe away a trailing bramble and said, 'Why?'

'Because we need it,' Ben told her. 'That's why.''

'We need a tank?'

'Unless *you* have a better plan?'

'*You* don't have a plan,' Maria told him. 'But that's fine, because neither do I. So let's go find a tank.'

Now that it would have been useful, the sound of the tanks' engines had all but died away. They fought their way along a narrowing avenue of greenery. Pale leaves glowed where the sun was struggling to break through.

The sound was muffled, but Ben could hear an engine. He saw the exhaust smoke before he saw the tank. It was buried in a mound of moss and overgrown vegetation – as if it had been standing there for years, not minutes.

'Waiting for something?' Maria wondered. She was whispering, as if afraid the tank – or the plants – might hear.

They picked their way closer. Maria hacked away

hanging creepers and chopped through a root that reared up in front of Ben, preparing the strike.

'Growl said the tanks were going to take the Green Man's influence with them, out of the village,' Ben said. 'Maybe it's getting its strength up to do just that.'

As they edged closer, they could see that the blanket of ragged green covering the tank had not grown up round it. It was spilling out of the open hatch on the top. Twists of ivy and other weeds curled out of the end of the gun, while brambles and bindweed wrapped themselves along the barrel.

Ben reached up and grabbed one of the trembling weeds that were poking out of the gun. It snapped between his fingers.

'It's brittle.'

'All the plants are getting brittle.' Maria swung her sword in a low arc, snapping through a variety of branches and stems to make the point. 'There's not enough water in the soil to support the sudden growth.'

'Dry and brittle,' Ben said thoughtfully.

'What are you thinking?' Maria asked.

Her face was shadowed, stained green by the filtered light. It made her look even more moody and sullen than usual.

'I'm wondering if you can drive a tank,' Ben said. 'That way at least we can get through the jungle.'

Maria's sullenness was gone in an instant. 'I'll give it a go.' She paused to hack away a fern that lashed out from the shadows. 'But we need to evict the current occupants first.'

The note of the engine changed, deepening as they approached. The tracks began to move – slowly eating into the mossy ground, wrenching out the tangled plants that were wound into the metal sections of the track and the wheels.

'It's moving!' Ben shouted above the increasing noise.

'Yeah, I noticed.'

Ben ran, his feet sinking into the spongy ground. It seemed that the earth itself was pulling at his ankles. He was heading for the back of the tank as it started to move away.

Ahead of him, Maria grabbed hold of an overhanging creeper with her free hand, swinging herself up on to the thick branch of an ancient oak tree. She ran along the branch. Leaves grabbed at her, while smaller limbs whipped across. The branch itself began to twist and buck under her feet. She ignored all this and jumped, landing sure-footed as a cat on the back of the tank. She bent her knees to absorb the force of the drop, bringing her sword up at once, then chopping down on a tangle of long grasses and bindweed that hurled itself at her.

Gathering speed, the tank began to pull away from Ben. It was now or never. As he ran faster, he could feel his heart thumping, his legs straining. He jumped for the back of the tank.

Maria's hand grabbed hold of his wrist as he fell just short. She wrenched him up beside her with a strength born of desperation and adrenalin. Ben stood there gasping as she hacked away at the writhing plants.

'They certainly know we're here,' Maria yelled above the straining engine. 'What now, Mastermind?'

Ben pointed at the open turret of the tank, where a green shape was heaving itself out, growing so rapidly it looked as if it would swamp them. Maria seemed to understand and hacked a way across the back of the tank towards the rising mass of green.

As soon as she was within range, she swung the sword hard at the leafy pillar forcing its way up from the hatch. The blade bit deep. Branches and leaves fell away. But they were replaced almost at once by more.

'I can't cut away everything,' Maria shouted at Ben.

'You don't have to,' he shouted back.

The expression on Maria's face when she saw what Ben was holding was a mixture of surprise, disbelief and elation. Her look made the whole nightmare almost worthwhile. He raised the flare pistol and hurled himself into the midst of the green mass.

The plants scratched and clawed at his face and hands, tore at his clothes. Only as he reached deep into the foliage, struggling to keep hold of the pistol, did Ben realise he didn't have a clue what he was doing. Knight had said it was loaded. But did it need priming or anything? Was there a safety catch?

His index finger was tight against the trigger. He squeezed. It didn't move – nothing. He was struggling to keep hold of the pistol, scrabbling with his other hand to try to find a mechanism, a lever, anything that might move or twist or click to make it work. All the time, stems and shoots were tearing at his hands, trying to drag away the pistol.

Finally, he found something that moved – at the back. A cocking lever, maybe? He couldn't hold on any longer. A length of bramble was cutting into his throat, squeezing tight. Maria was holding on to his legs – the only reason he'd not been dragged bodily into the tank. He tugged at the trigger and felt it give.

Then the flare pistol was jolted from his grasp.

Ben struggled back out of the greenery. He'd failed. He'd pulled the trigger and nothing had happened.

Or had it?

Even above the engine noise, he heard the whoosh of the flare as it ignited in the cabin. Ben leaned forward again to see what was happening. It was a mistake. Immediately the greenery pouring out of the tank enveloped him, dragging him down.

17

A SUDDEN LIGHT EXPLODED IN FRONT OF BEN. A rush of heat, brighter and angrier than the sun. The branches holding him withered in a moment, shrinking back. They shrivelled and burned.

He hurled himself backwards and knocked straight into Maria. She grabbed him tight, stopping them both from falling.

A ball of flame erupted from the open hatch on the tank's turret. It blasted upwards and outwards. Fire ran like liquid across the shell of the vehicle. A wall of flame rolled towards them. The ground on all sides was on fire. Green became red and orange and yellow, with black smoke billowing out. Branches fell, creepers sagged, plants were engulfed as the tracked fireball roared through the jungle.

With nowhere else to go, Ben and Maria threw themselves forward, into the flames – and out the other side. The tank had been burned clean. The dark metal was smoking. Charred remains of the vegetation emerged from the hatch like blackened bones. Ben could feel the heat through his shoes. He had to keep moving so as not to get burned. His clothes were steaming.

Together they ran for the hatch. Inside the fire had died down, but the interior of the tank was filled with smoke. The vehicle continued undeterred, crashing through the undergrowth. It lurched violently upwards as it hit something. Stone crunched and shattered like sugar lumps under the tracks.

A tombstone.

They were in the churchyard.

Through a sudden clearing in the jungle, the church tower loomed ominously against the smoky sky. The fire on the tank had all but burned out. The plants around had stopped burning too. A blackened trail followed the tank as it tore through the vegetation. It was only going at walking pace, but nothing was about to stop it. The statue of an angel was knocked aside, wings crumbling. More gravestones shattered.

The smoke inside the tank was thinning a bit. Maria's eyes were shining – from excitement, or maybe from the stinging smoke. She pointed down through the hatch.

'Guide me,' she shouted.

'You know how to steer this thing?' Ben asked, staring at her.

'No. But it's got to be easier than trying to stop it.' She lowered herself quickly through the hatch. The remains of the plants inside shattered as she touched them, crumbling to powdered charcoal.

Ben leaned down into the tank. The cabin was a blackened mess. He was amazed how cramped the space inside the large vehicle seemed. Maria was strapping herself into one of the seats and reaching for the charred controls. There were small windows at the front through which she could look out, but she couldn't see much more than the thrashing foliage all around them as the tank forced its way through.

The whole vehicle lurched sideways.

'We've hit something!' Ben shouted.

The tank lurched the other way.

'No, we haven't. That was me,' Maria shouted back. 'I've got it now. Tell me which way to go.'

Ben looked up, searching for a glimpse of the church tower through the canopy of green.

Sam was crouching down at the other side of

the hatch. 'Over there.' She pointed across to the left of the tank.

'Left!' Ben yelled into the cabin.

'How much left?'

'Just . . . left. I'll say when to stop.'

The tank lurched sideways again, knocking Sam over. She picked herself up. 'Driven a lot of tanks, has she?'

'I think she's still learning.'

They crashed through more greenery and bumped over a fallen tree.

'Too far,' Ben called to Maria. 'Back a bit. Just a bit though. Maybe five degrees,' he added, looking at Sam to see if that sounded about right.

Maria's voice was faint and muffled. 'How much is five degrees, Mastermind?'

The tank was realigning, more evenly this time.

'About that much,' Ben agreed. 'Just keep going forward.'

Small trees and bushes folded down and crunched under the tracks. Chunks of broken gravestone went flying. Branches and leaves whipped over Ben and Sam as they clung to the top of the tank. It seemed to be picking up speed.

'Right a bit more,' Sam told Ben.

He called to Maria and she corrected the tank.

The tower loomed huge above them, blotting out the sky – much larger than the tank. They were so close that Ben could see the cracks in the ancient, weathered stonework. He could see the weeds and moss and stonecrop and tufts of grass embedded in the crumbling mortar.

He could see the carved faces of the Green Man snarling in anger – in sudden horror as they saw the heavy tank smashing through the last barriers between them.

'I don't think we want to be on the top here,' Sam shouted to Ben.

She was right. They were hurtling at the tower, gathering more and more speed.

'Time to get out,' Ben shouted through the hatch.

'No way!' Maria yelled back. 'I have to hold it steady or it veers off. And anyway, there's no time.'

She looked over her shoulder and Ben saw her face was set in an expression of determination and exhilaration.

'You jump,' she told him. 'I'm staying here.'

He could tell there was no point in arguing with her. Sam was no longer there – maybe she'd jumped or maybe she'd just . . . gone.

With no time to see what he'd be landing on, Ben leapt from the top of the tank. He rolled as he hit the ground, tangling in a mass of undergrowth and knocking his shoulder painfully against a tombstone.

He came to a halt and looked up to see the tank plough into the tower.

It smashed through the corner of the building, sending stones and mortar flying. For a while, the tank kept going, forcing its way through the building. But then it slowed. The engine was straining, the tracks caught in roots and rubble. The massive tower was leaning to one side. But it remained standing.

The carved heads stared down at Ben. Even though he couldn't make out their expressions, he could feel their hatred.

'Maria,' Ben breathed.

She was trapped in the tank, which was buried in the side of the tower. With the weight of the building crushing down on the turret, there was no way was she ever getting out.

'Ben, are you OK?' Gemma struggled out of the tangled undergrowth in front of him.

Rupam was close behind her. 'Where's Maria?' he gasped.

In answer, Ben could only point at the tank jutting out from the church tower. As he pointed, the building trembled. A shower of stone fragments fell from the already ruined top of the tower, clattering across the back of the tank.

The sound of the tank's engine deepened. Ben could imagine Maria inside, trapped, hearing the rattle of stones on the roof and struggling to get moving again.

The tank inched forward. The tracks tore into the rubble beneath, finally getting some purchase and easing the vehicle forward.

As it moved, the tower above shook. More stones fell – larger chunks and blocks. A gargoyle crashed down, shattering to pieces on the side of the tank. Slowly but surely, though, the heavy vehicle was pulling clear – and the tower was collapsing as it did so.

The whole thing happened in slow motion. The tank pulling away. Black fumes streaming from the exhausts. The tower leaning, tipping. The stones at the top falling – the effect travelling down the length of the structure as it crashed down.

Ben and the others turned away. They covered their heads with their hands and arms as fragments of stone flew past them. Choking dust rose like smoke, clogging their eyes and throats, and the roar of the tank was lost in the rumble of the collapsing building.

All around, the trees and plants were in a frenzy. It was like a gale was blowing through the bizarre jungle, fanning the fire started when Ben had let off the flare. Nothing was still. A noise like shrieking or screaming filled the air.

A stone head rolled across the ground close to Ben. A screaming face surrounded by leaves. It stared at him accusingly and he realised that they hadn't won yet – the grotesque creature still had power.

A rusty, broken shovel slammed down into the face, splitting the ancient carving with a screech of metal on stone. Growl lifted the shovel from the debris. Knight stood beside him.

'We must find them all and break them,' Growl said. 'Just as Greene broke the statues of the saints. It seems that destroying the tower didn't work, so the only way to destroy the power of the Green Man is to break up the images of him.'

The ground was covered with rubble from the tower. One half of it had collapsed completely, the other was a stunted, ragged ruin.

'You find the carved heads in the rubble,' Knight told Ben and the others. 'Growl and I will get the ones still on the tower.' He glanced at the battered tank, which had slewed to a halt some metres away. 'And see if Maria's all right.'

There were two carved heads lying close together nearby. Ben tried not to look as he brought a heavy lump of stone down on one of them. It shattered at his second blow. Rupam smashed the other head repeatedly with another piece of stone from the ruins.

The falling tower had cleared the immediate area of plants. But away from the devastation, the greenery was thrashing angrily. The fires were dying down, beaten out by the dense undergrowth.

'What else can happen?' Rupam said, seeing Ben and Gemma's anxious looks.

'I don't want to find out,' Ben told him. 'Let's just smash these stone heads and be done with it.'

But Gemma's gasp brought his attention back to the circle of green. 'The Green Man.'

One whole section of vegetation was gathering, growing, forming into a massive figure. It stood over three metres high. Leaves wove round its head, while stems and branches jutted from its body. The hands were wooden stumps, with leafy fingers sprouting out. Although made from roots and branches, leaves and stems, it was recognisably Colonel Greene. His huge face echoed the foliate heads that had been round the tower. It twisted in rage as the figure tore itself free of the plants and trees and started across the sea of rubble towards Ben, Rupam and Gemma.

'Find the rest of the heads,' Ben said. 'We have to smash them before it gets to us.'

Climbing over the remains of the tower, Knight and Growl had seen what was happening. Knight took the shovel from Growl and prised a foliate head away from its alcove. It fell to the ground, shattering to pieces as it hit the rubble-strewn ground below. He reached across for the next of the heads.

'Here's one!' Gemma shouted.

She hammered at it with a stone, but wasn't strong enough to break it. Rupam ran to help.

'Ben, over here,' he called.

But Ben was staring at the nightmare figure lurching towards them. 'We have to destroy that too,' he realised. 'We have to kill the Green Man.'

There would be a flare pistol in the tank. Just like the one he'd got from the other tank with Knight. Ben was running before he'd even consciously thought of that. His ankle twisted painfully on the uneven rubble, but he kept going. Maria was hauling herself out of the tank turret. She looked shaken and pale. When she saw what was coming after Ben, her eyes widened in shock and horror.

'Flare pistol,' he yelled. 'In the kit box inside the turret!'

Maria disappeared inside the tank again.

The massive creature was stomping after Ben. It howled in inarticulate fury. A huge arm reached out for him, shoots erupting from the stubby green fingers, growing rapidly into creepers.

He managed to avoid them and kept running, clambering over a pile of stones and up on to the back of the tank.

'Flare pistol!' he yelled again.

'There isn't one,' Maria told him, emerging again from the hatch.

'There is – there has to be.'

She ducked inside again as Ben followed her and dropped down into the cabin. He could see the box fixed on the inside wall. And he could see that it was open – the flare pistol gone. Ben felt a sudden punch of panic and disbelief. This was the *same* tank that he and Knight had been in earlier. The flare pistol was gone because he had already taken it.

'I think we have a problem,' Maria said, and the calmness with which she spoke was worrying – as if she was resigned to their fate.

Through the narrow observation window at

the front of the tank, Ben saw the huge figure of the Green Man standing right in front of them, less than ten metres away. The hideous face was twisted in unnatural laughter.

Ben and Maria were both frozen with fear. The only movement was the Green Man stepping towards them. And a flicker of light on the charred instrument panel in front of Ben.

Maria saw it at the same moment. A flicker of red under the black residue of the fire. A button, the protective cover that usually hid it standing open – as if the button was about to be pressed when the flare burned away the plants that were driving the tank and shelling the village.

Ben's finger hit the button at the same moment as Maria's. They both pressed hard. They both felt the tank shudder. They both heard the roar of the gun above them.

And they both watched through the observation window as the shell of depleted uranium hit the green figure. It exploded on his chest, the sudden fireball rippling out. In an instant the creature was engulfed in an inferno. The limbs fell away, still burning. Fire raged through the body, erupting from the screaming mouth and hollow eyes.

Behind the falling mass of flame stood the

shattered remains of the church tower. As the fireball consumed the last of the Green Man and burned itself out, Knight raised the last of the foliate heads and dashed it against the side of the ruined tower wall. It shattered into pieces.

On the far side of the devastation, another tank appeared. It pushed through the trees and slowed to a halt. Already the vegetation was drawing back from its dark, brutal exterior. All around, the greenery was dying down. What had been a jungle was again just an overgrown graveyard, beside a ruined church and the collapsed remains of a tower.

Ben climbed out of the tank, reaching back to help Maria after him.

'Look,' she said, staring past Ben. 'Look at the other tank.'

He turned to see what she meant. The tank was again covered with plants. But it wasn't the unforgiving greenery of leaves and wood, brambles and thorns. Spilling from the hatch and dripping from the barrel of the gun, laced through the tracks and wheels, was a mass of colour – reds and yellows, blues and pinks. The tank was covered with flowers.

18

THERE WAS A BUZZ AMONG THE CHILDREN back at Gibbet Manor. Most were due to leave in a few days, their education complete – for now, at least.

A tall, thin boy with dark hair and glasses pushed past Ben at lunch. The same boy Ben had been sure was sneering at him. Was it only a week ago? It seemed like a lifetime.

'Hey,' Ben complained.

'Oh, hey,' the boy replied, turning and coming back. 'Sorry, I was miles away. There's just so much to think about. So much to take in, you know.'

Ben nodded. 'Tell me about it.' He waited for the sneer to return, or a sarky comment about how Ben must know it all anyway.

But instead the boy smiled. A proper, genuine smile. 'Sorry,' he said. 'I guess it's all old news to you. It's been so great having you and Rupam here, treating us like we might match up to you one day. I mean, we're just passing through and you guys – you're on the front line. All the time. Everyone says how hard it must be and, well . . .' He shrugged, suddenly looking embarrassed. 'Thanks,' he finished. 'Thanks for everything.'

Ben watched the boy leave. He didn't even remember his name.

The new kids started a week later. Ben and Sam stood at Ben's window and watched them arrive in a minibus from Plymouth station. Their parents – and most of their teachers – thought they were on an Outward Bound course, and when they returned they'd have pictures and stories to prove it. But they would be from two days, not two weeks, out on the moor. A survival course of a very different sort from the one their parents imagined.

That evening, Ben was summoned to Knight's study. He and Sam went in, apprehensive. Was he in trouble?

But Gemma, Maria and Rupam were there already. There was another boy too. He looked nervous, blushing beneath a scattering of freckles. His hair was a mess of blond thatch.

'I wanted you all to meet someone,' Knight said.

'This is Tommy. It's because of him that we all had such a fun time in Templeton.'

'Thanks, Tommy,' Maria said. 'It was a blast.'

The boy frowned, not sure if he was being teased.

'It's because of Tommy that matters didn't get out of hand,' Knight said. 'We have to thank you for being so alert and getting us involved.' He shook the embarrassed boy by the hand.

They all thanked him and shook his hand, and Tommy had managed a grin by the time he left them.

'So, it's all over,' Ben said.

'Not exactly,' Knight said. 'That's partly why I wanted to talk to you all. Captain Morton has a few things to smooth out with the army. Webby was watching it all on the satellite and has shown me the time-lapse images. When you destroyed the tower, the vegetation had already overrun the rest of the village and was spreading outwards. So well done, everyone.'

'All in a day's work,' Rupam said.

'What did he mean, "not exactly"?' Sam whispered to Ben.

'You said it wasn't exactly all over,' Ben said out loud.

'The Crystal,' Knight said. He looked at them each carefully in turn.

'What about it?' Gemma asked. 'You put it in your pocket.'

Knight nodded. 'And when I got back here, I had Webby run some tests on it.'

'Is it Diablo's Crystal?' Rupam asked. 'One of the artefacts?'

'Oh, yes. Without it, Carstairs Endeavour could never hope to successfully summon forth Mortagula and control him.'

'So what's the problem?' Ben asked.

'You don't know?'

Ben shook his head.

'No, I don't think you do.' Knight turned to Rupam. 'What about you?'

'Sorry?'

'Or you?' Knight turned suddenly to ask Maria. She blinked in surprise, but did not reply. 'And you?' Knight asked Gemma quietly.

Gemma shook her head. She glanced over at a large glass-fronted cabinet fixed to the wall – the securely locked cabinet where Knight kept many of his souvenirs and relics. 'It's gone, hasn't it? I know – I could *feel* it. And now . . . Nothing.'

Knight nodded gravely. 'Yes, the Crystal has gone.'

'But how?' Ben asked. 'I mean, did it just vanish or . . .'

'Or did someone take it?' Sam finished for him.

Ben didn't echo her words. Even though they could not have heard them, everyone in the room would be thinking the same thing.

'Something for me to sort out,' Knight said. 'But it is worrying, to say the least. And as you know, not the first time we've had a problem. I must ask Mrs Bailey to review our defences and alarms. But perhaps its purpose was done and it has simply dissolved. Let's pray we never find out otherwise. Now . . .' He clapped his hands together, but Ben could see the anxiety in his expression. 'I must officially welcome the new batch of students.'

'So you're not the new boy any more,' Rupam told Ben as they left the study.

'I suppose not.'

'Of course not,' Gemma agreed.

'You're one of us now,' Maria said. 'For better or for worse.' Her sullen face suggested 'worse'. 'One of the team.'

Ben watched them head off for the common room. 'Whatever that means,' he murmured.

Sam was standing beside him. 'You know what it means,' she said. 'It means that this is where the fun *really* starts.'